STEP ON A CRACK

SPINETINGLERS

#9

STEP ON A CRACK

M. T. COFFIN

AN AVON CAMELOT BOOK

STEP ON A CRACK is an original publication of Avon Books. This work has never before appeared in book form.

AVON BOOKS
A division of
The Hearst Corporation
1350 Avenue of the Americas
New York, New York 10019

Copyright © 1996 by C. J. Henderson
Excerpt from *The Dead Kid Did It* copyright © 1996 by George Edward Stanley
Published by arrangement with the author
Library of Congress Catalog Card Number: 95-95106
ISBN: 0-380-78432-7
RL: 4.9

First Avon Camelot Printing: May 1996

CAMELOT TRADEMARK REG. U.S. PAT. OFF. AND IN OTHER COUNTRIES, MARCA REGISTRADA, HECHO EN U.S.A.

Printed in the U.S.A.

OPM 10 9 8 7 6 5 4 3 2 1

650 YEARS AGO

PROLOGUE

Running. Running fast.

It was the only chance they had.

"Leave!" screamed the chief. "Leave now."

The old man stood his ground in the center of the tribe's canvas lodges. With his longest war spear in his hand—the one given to him by his father—he commanded his people, "Run to the mountains."

The air was filled with the burning smell. It meant that the thing was coming again. It meant that it was there already.

And then the warrior chief saw the grass moving. The thing that had killed eight of his finest warriors—swallowed them whole—was coming for him.

"All of you," he shouted in a clear, loud voice as he raised his spear. "Run."

3

The thing tore up the ground between itself and the chief, heading straight toward him. The grass withered at its touch—dying instantly. The chief did not move.

He waited for the monster, holding his war spear above his head. Ready to drive his weapon into the horror under the earth, he called out once more, "Run!"

And then the monster reached the chief. As several of his people turned, they saw their leader disappear, sucked down into the ground like all the others. The only thing left behind was his father's spear.

His people did not see what took him, only the bloody spray that filled the air when he disappeared.

Everyone ran. None of them doubted that they had only one chance left.

Running as far as they could. As fast as they could.

All the surviving members of the Taranka tribe ran from their village as swiftly as possible. None except the smallest children carried anything. They did not bother with blankets or weapons or even food.

They could find more food. They could weave more blankets. And weapons . . . as their warriors and their chief had shown, weapons could not help them against the thing in the center of their village.

Nothing could stand against the spirit of death that had invaded their lives. Those who survived would mark the outer boundaries of their former home.

They would leave signs for others who might follow them, warning them of the terror that lurked in the lush valley near the lake.

They would find a way to bind the horrible beast to the land, and they would watch over it, making sure it never came forth again.

But the surviving members of the Taranka tribe would never return to their lands. Not for their animals, their clothing, the stores of seeds and tools . . . none of it.

Ever.

Now it all belonged to the invisible killer beneath the grass.

After a few days, the thing realized all its potential victims were gone. Lurking beneath the ground, it cursed itself. It had been too hungry, too greedy. It had wanted—needed—the raw warmth of their souls too much to kill one victim at a time.

Now it had driven all its prey away. The Indians had fled into the mountains where it could not follow.

The thing screamed in rage—black with anger that it had been so stupid.

After a few years, however, its anger passed. It knew that sooner or later, men would return to the valley. Sooner or later, they would come back with their oh-so-tasty souls, and the thing under the grass would feed again.

And, it told itself, *next time,* it would be more careful. Next time, it would hunt quietly. Next time, it would not be so greedy.

It would work slowly until it had regained its former power. It would kill slowly, sucking soul after soul until it had stored up enough energy to again move from planet to planet.

But for now, it would sleep. Its chance would come again. And then—when it did—the monster in the ground would drain all life from the Earth. It would suck in the souls of everyone on the planet and be on its way.

It had spent too much time here already.

NOW

I

"Hey, watch out," shouted Danny. "You know what they say—'Step on a crack, break your mother's back.'"

"Oh, yeah," Billy answered. "Right."

Billy Carne looked down at his foot. It was resting right on the long black line of tar separating two blocks of sidewalk. Yeah, sure—okay. His foot was on the crack.

So what?

Having turned ten years old last month, he was far too mature to believe in babyish sayings.

Billy was tall for his age, a good-looking boy with wavy, sandy-colored hair and brown eyes. He was the leader of his group of friends. Every day, the five of them followed the same routine.

First, Billy would stop at Danny Hawkes's house. Danny was his best friend—had been since first grade. After that, they would meet the rest of their pals on the next block and continue on to school.

Danny was definitely the group's main clown. He always came up with the best jokes—like pointing out the crack Billy was stepping on. Still teasing his friend, Danny punched Billy on the arm, saying, "Oh, wow—look at this, guys. I don't believe it. Carne hates his mom."

"I do not," snapped Billy. He realized Danny was only teasing, but he slapped his friend's hand away anyway, telling him, "What I hate is immature geekballs who still act like they're in second grade."

The other guys laughed. Every day, Billy and Danny would come up with some reason to goof on each other. Their friends knew this was only the beginning. As they expected, Danny attacked again, saying, "It's okay. I understand."

"You understand what?"

"You're just tense today," answered Danny. "I mean, it is today you were going to ask Sheila Knisbaum to go to the movies, isn't it?"

"Sheila Knisbaum?" asked Billy. The other boys in the group started to snicker and to call out things like "Oh, no, gross," and "Billy's in love."

Sheila was the cutest girl in the school. Absolutely the cutest. But she was also the daughter of the toughest teacher in school. Nobody had ever had the nerve to ask her out. Danny asked, "Wasn't it today?"

While the others guys laughed, Billy smiled and said, "Heck, no. I asked her out last week."

Everyone got quiet. Even Danny. They all knew Billy was just teasing Danny back, but they still wanted to hear what he was going to say. When Billy didn't say anything else, however, Danny was forced to ask, "Yeah? So, what did she say?"

"She said she was saving all her kisses for you."

Everyone laughed.

Even Danny had to give in and laugh at that one. Of course, he made spitting sounds and kept wiping at his mouth, pretending to be getting rid of Sheila's kisses. But he admitted it was pretty funny. Once everyone was done kidding around, Jack Harris, one of the other boys, said, "Do you guys think we're all going to be able to make it to the roof today?"

Everyone knew what he meant. Today in gym class, Mr. Worster was going to make them climb the rope that went all the way to the gymnasium ceiling.

11

It didn't matter to any of them that every year, all the fifth grade boys had to climb the rope. None of them believed it actually could be done.

"I don't know, Jack," Billy admitted. "It sure looks like a long way to the top from down on the floor."

"Yeah," agreed Mike Morgan. "Like about a mile."

"Aw, come on," snapped Danny. "You guys are being babies about this."

"Are not," Jack answered. "We just said it looks hard, is all. And it does."

"Oh, so what?" Danny asked. "So big deal if we can't climb the dumb rope. What's Worster going to do? Fail us?"

"I don't know," answered Jack quietly. He hated when Danny started in on him. He wasn't as quick as Billy. Not caring that he was making Jack uncomfortable, Danny continued.

"I mean, is he going to keep us in the fifth grade an extra year? Is he going to have big red marks put in our permanent records—'Don't give this guy a job. He can't climb a stupid rope.'"

"I don't know," mumbled Jack. "How do I know?"

"I do," said Danny. "I heard that he has a branding iron that he heats up and he brands

12

all the guys who can't do it. Big letters across their foreheads—I COULDN'T CLIMB THE ROPE. You only get one chance. If you can't do it . . . sssssssssssssssss . . . right in the head."

"That's just stupid," snapped Malcomb Gettle. He was the heaviest of them all, and the most concerned about being able to climb the rope. Malcomb squeezed his lips together hard, then opened them, saying, "That's the stupidest thing I ever heard. If he did that, there'd be guys all over town with I COULDN'T CLIMB THE ROPE burned in their heads."

Danny smiled, then said, "I think they all moved after they got branded."

"Oh, that's it," shouted Jack. Letting his book bag slide down off his shoulders, Jack swung the pack as hard as he could, hitting Danny in the side.

Danny laughed. He loved to tell stories that were so crazy he made the other guys nuts. He kept dodging as Jack swung again and again, laughing as he said, "Don't take it out on me because you're going to have a forehead full of words."

Finally, Billy caught Jack's hand, stopping him from swinging at Danny anymore.

13

"Forget it," he told Jack. "You're going to end up spilling your books."

As all the boys settled down, they turned the corner onto Munsen Street. Munsen was the street their school was on, so, of course, they slowed down automatically. After all, none of them wanted to get to school any faster than they had to. As they walked, Danny said, "I'll tell you, I don't know about this rope climbing stuff."

"What do you mean?" asked Malcomb.

"I mean, really . . . what do we need to know how to climb a rope for? Okay, I understand taking English. You've got to be able to read the newspaper to look for a job, and to find out what time movies are, and stuff like that. And you need math to be able to make sure no one cheats you when you're paying for things, and doing your taxes and all."

Everyone nodded his head in agreement. As they did, Danny kept talking. "But, I mean, will somebody tell me when I'm going to need to climb a rope? I'm not Tarzan, you know. I don't live in the jungle. I'm not going to go to work on the treetop expressway."

All the guys chuckled.

"This is the modern world. If I want to get to the top of a building, I'll take the elevator. Or an

14

escalator, or the stairs. Or a ladder. But, I mean, come on. Climbing rope? Would someone tell me when any of us—*any of us*—is ever going to need that particular skill?"

"This afternoon," Billy answered. A big smile crossed his face as he added, "In gym class."

All the boys chuckled. And then the first bell sounded just as they arrived at the entrance to the school. Hurrying onward in between the two large brick pillars of the front gate, none of them really noticed the slight tremor that shook the sidewalk.

Maybe they were distracted by the bell. Maybe they were just in too big a hurry. Whatever the case, they missed all the little clues. Like the slight burning smell in the air . . . The shudder passing through the ground that made the grass on both sides of the pathway rustle . . . The crumbs of cement along all the cracks in the sidewalk that seemed to leap up and bounce about for no reason . . . The hungry sound that growled ever so faintly beneath the earth.

The hungry, hungry sound.

"Climb, maggot."

Mr. Worster stood at the bottom of the rope. Malcomb Gettle hung halfway from the top, panting. Sweat poured off his forehead, filling his eyes. Suddenly, his legs slipped loose from around the rope. Blinded by the sweat in his eyes, his arms aching, he thrashed back and forth, trying to get his legs locked around the rope again.

Mr. Worster steadied the rope at the bottom, shouting up at Malcomb. "I said, *climb*. Let go with one hand, shove it up, grab on, and then do it again. Do it, Mr. Gettle. *Do it!*"

Malcomb could feel the sweat stinging his eyes, trying to force him to cry. I won't cry, he thought. I won't. I won't. Forcing his eyes open, he stared up at the ceiling so far away, thinking, You can't make me cry, Mr. Worster. Nobody can.

16

And then Malcomb clamped his teeth together and started to climb again.

On the gymnasium floor, the rest of the class watched him start to move once more. Most of them had already had their turn. Jack and Mike had both made it to the stripe of paint that marked the three-quarter point—a passing grade. That had been enough for them.

Danny had passed that point, going on another yard. He had slipped then, and Mr. Worster had told him to come back down before he got himself killed. Now only Malcomb and Billy were left.

Everyone watched Malcomb. Even guys that didn't really like him were watching—quietly. Hoping he'd make it. Some were even praying for him. It didn't matter what kids thought of each other outside of school—they all knew that inside it was them against the teachers.

Mr. Worster was almost as tough as Mr. Knisbaum.

And twice as scary.

"Climb, Mr. Gettle—you sack of rocks. Two more feet. I can see it from here. Two lousy feet."

Malcomb gasped for breath. The sweat on his hands made him feel like he was going to slip.

"Climb—climb—*climb!*"

He slid his left hand up a few inches. He had

17

no idea how high he was. The sweat pouring off his head had forced him to shut his eyes again.

"Do it, Mr. Gettle. Do it." Worster shouted out to everyone else in the class, "Tell him. Help him out. Give him the beat, you slugs."

"Do it, Malcomb," shouted Billy.

Danny was second, yelling, "Yeah, go on, tubby. Do it. Do it."

In seconds the entire class was shouting together, sending their encouragement upward to the swinging figure above them on the rope. "Do it, Malcomb, do it. Do it, Malcomb, do it . . ."

Praying for himself, Malcomb swallowed another gulp of air and then forced his right hand up as far as he could. Sweat dripped down his arms, his legs. Drops fell away from him one after another. Malcomb thought he could hear them hitting the mats far below.

"Do it, Malcomb, do it. Do it, Malcomb . . ."

Straining, he stretched his arm out as far as it would go, fumbling around for the rope. And then—suddenly—as his fingers found it—

"Awww-right!" He heard Danny screaming, "You did it, tubby! *You did it!*"

Malcomb's eyes popped open in amazement. The fingers of his right hand were half a foot past the paint mark.

18

"Get down here, Mr. Gettle," shouted the gym teacher. "Stop hogging the rope. Carne still wants to show us what he can do. Don't you, Mr. Carne?"

But, before Billy could answer, the shower bell rang. Mr. Worster turned to the class and told them to head on into the locker room, telling Billy, "Don't worry, Mr. Carne—you'll get your chance to show off for everyone first thing Monday morning." Then Mr. Worster turned his back on Billy, directing all his attention to helping Malcomb come back down the rope.

"Don't go too fast—you don't want to burn your hands or thighs, and you don't want to fall. Take it easy, Mr. Gettle. You did just fine. No need to hurry now."

Billy stood and listened as Mr. Worster talked Malcomb back down the rope. When his friend was only a dozen feet from the thick pile of mats underneath the rope, the teacher told him to go ahead and drop.

Malcomb let go of the rope and fell like a rock. He hit the mats so hard, dust came out of the ends of the ones on top. He didn't get hurt, though. Mr. Worster stuck out his hand and helped the boy to his feet. "You did real good today, Mr. Gettle," he told Malcomb.

19

"Better than you thought?" asked Malcomb, puffing and sweating.

"No," replied the teacher honestly. "I knew you could do it. Maybe just better than *you* thought."

Malcomb steadied himself and then let go of Mr. Worster's hand. The teacher told him, "You take a good shower. I'll write you a note for your next class."

"Thank you," said Malcomb. Then, as the two turned toward the shower room, they saw Billy standing there—waiting. The gym teacher yelled, "And what can we do for you?"

"Mr. Worster—I've just got study hall next. I thought if I did my climb now, you'd be able to put the rope away. You know—so we could do something else on Monday?"

Mr. Worster sent Malcomb running for the showers, then asked Billy, "Okay. Your pal's gone. Now spill it. What's this all about?"

Billy swallowed. He stared at the teacher without blinking for a long moment, then finally said, "Well, I—ah, I guess, er . . . what I mean is . . . I was really psyched to do this today. I'd just feel, I don't know, like better or something, if I could go ahead and get it over with."

Worster looked at Billy for a long moment, then finally said, "Who am I to stand in your way?" Bowing, he pointed to the rope as he said, "You want to climb . . . climb."

Billy moved forward. Walking past Mr. Worster, he jumped up, catching hold of the rope and locking his legs around it at the same time. The gym teacher grabbed the bottom of the rope as it began to whip around.

Malcomb watched from the locker room doorway. Billy Carne was the boy he most wanted to be like. He was proud of himself for having made the three-quarter mark on the rope.

But he knew he would have never volunteered to climb the rope as Billy had just done. Not in a thousand years. Not in a million.

"Okay," said Mr. Worster. "You're doing pretty good, Mr. Carne. Keep that even pace and keep your legs locked. Don't drag them—you'll scrape all the skin off your knees. But don't let them unlock."

The gym teacher kept one hand on the rope, stretching out as far as he could so he could watch Billy's progress. Not thinking about his teacher, the boy just kept climbing. More than a third of the way up the rope, Billy thought, I can do this. I can do it.

Below him, Mr. Worster echoed his thoughts. "That's it, Mr. Carne. You can do this. Just one hand after another. One hand after another. Breathe and climb. Breathe and climb."

Breathe and climb, thought Billy. Breathe and climb.

"Good work," shouted the teacher. "You're already past the halfway mark. Now, just keep going like you are. Nice and easy does it."

Billy was just starting to breathe heavy, just a bit. He was beginning to feel his arms as well, just a bit.

"Three-quarters, Mr. Carne. You've passed. You can stop any time."

"When I run out of rope, Mr. Worster."

"Whatever," answered the teacher. He smiled as he added, "You can do it twice if you like."

"Oh, no thank you, sir," shouted Billy. Trying not to laugh, he took a deep breath and yelled, "I wouldn't want to be *too* late for study hall."

And then his hand touched the roof of the gymnasium. Taking another deep breath, he shouted, "Good enough, Mr. Worster?"

"Good enough, Mr. Carne. Now get your show-off butt back down here."

Billy started down the rope again, moving smoothly hand over hand. When he was only six feet from the mats, he dropped lightly to the floor. As they both headed for the locker room, the gym teacher said, "That was good climbing, Mr. Carne. Couldn't have been better, really."

"Thank you," answered Billy.

"Yeah, sure," said his teacher. "But you mind if I ask you a question?"

"No," answered Billy. "What is it?"

"Sure—not having to drag the mats out and get the rope unhooked from the ceiling on Monday is good news for me, and I thank you for getting this out of the way."

"No problem," said Billy.

"Yeah. But if you would—tell me the *real* reason *why* you wanted to do this today." Before Billy could say anything, Mr. Worster added, "I saw the look in your eyes. I don't know why, but you wanted to climb today for some reason other than helping out your poor old gym teacher."

"Well," said Billy, not really sure of his answer, "I don't know what to say. I was pretty sure I could climb the rope and all. No sweat. You know what I mean?"

"Yeah," answered Mr. Worster. "I didn't have any doubt you could do it. So what made it so important?"

Billy stopped walking. Turning to his teacher, he tried to put into words what he had been feeling all morning. "Well, you see, when I was com-

ing into school this morning with the guys . . .
just when we came through the gate, I . . . I don't
know . . . I just got this *feeling* that it was important to be *sure* I could climb the rope." Billy
paused. All of a sudden he felt silly—stupid.
Without looking at Mr. Worster, he asked, "Do
you know what I mean?"

"Makes perfect sense to me, Mr. Carne."

Billy let out the breath of air he'd been holding.
He didn't know how his teacher could know what
he was feeling, but he didn't care. Ever since he
had entered the school that morning, he'd been
growing more and more nervous about the rope
climb—or something. He'd been feeling almost
scared, as if his life depended on being able to
climb a rope. Now he felt much better.

As Mr. Worster headed for his office, he told
Billy to come back and get a note for his study
hall teacher. The boy said, "Sure," and then made
the turn that led to the showers. When he did,
he found Malcomb waiting for him.

"You made it."

"Yeah, easy," answered Billy. "But so did you.
Good going. I told you you could do it."

"I know," said Malcomb. "Thanks." As the two
boys continued toward the showers, Malcomb
asked, "Hey, you know what you told Worster,

about feeling funny when we were just getting to school?"

"Yeah . . . ?"

"And how you wanted to climb just to make sure you could do it?"

Billy nodded.

"I just wanted to tell you . . . I felt the same thing."

And then Malcomb ran for the showers, leaving Billy feeling a little confused. Billy watched him disappear around the corner without knowing what to say.

It was one thing to feel weird about something. That could mean anything. But it was another thing when someone else felt the same way. That felt scary.

Real scary.

3

"Hey, guys—they're going to pour the cement!"

Everyone ran toward Danny. They had all been going to the South Side of town every day after school for weeks, waiting for the construction workers to begin pouring the new cement. Now that it was about to happen, no one wanted to miss it. Especially not Billy.

Like almost every boy in the world, Billy loved construction sites and heavy machinery. He could name every type of earthmover, hauler, and ground breaker there was. He had questioned the construction crew constantly since the South Side rebuilding had begun.

In fact, the job foreman had said that Billy had asked so many questions, he probably knew as much about the big rigs as the foreman did. Everyone who heard him had laughed. All of the

26

local site workers liked Billy. None of them had minded answering any of his questions.

"Okay, you kids," called out the foreman. "You all back up some now."

Everyone scrambled back a few steps. Billy and his friends weren't the only ones there. A lot of other boys and girls from school had made the trip to the South Side of town every day just like them. They all wanted to watch the old buildings get torn down and the new ones go up.

A lot of their fathers had taken to driving by after work to pick the kids up. Some of them showed up every day. They all said they just wanted their kids to have a good time. Everyone knew the truth, though. All the dads wanted to watch what was going on as much as the kids did.

Billy thought back to the day the construction men had torn down the old Selby Tower. When his dad arrived, they had just started cutting away the steel support skeleton on the old fifteenth floor. The workers would cut through the heavy girders and braces and then push them to the ground below.

His dad saw two hit at the same time. They smashed against each other, creating sparks and sending big dust clouds in the air. His dad had taken off his hat and stared upward, saying he wanted to see another one fall before they left.

After five minutes, another girder had fallen to the ground. It crashed into a pile of others. Rust flew into the air along with more sparks and more dust. Billy's dad decided he wanted to see that again.

And so they had stayed for another. And another. Then three more. Then ten more. Before Billy and his dad knew it, the workers were down to the thirteenth floor, and they were both late for dinner. They had rushed to the car then, hurrying home as fast as they could. His mom had been annoyed at them for being so late. She had forced him and his dad to apologize about five times. But they both thought it was worth it.

Billy thought about that day while he and his friends waited for the cement flow to start. He knew his dad would enjoy watching that and wished he could be there. Then, before he could check his watch to see if his dad might arrive in time to see the pouring, the foreman yelled, "Okay, Charlie—let it rip."

Charlie was a large balding man with a thick black beard. He had been standing at the back of the cement mixer waiting for the foreman's signal. He waved to the foreman to signal back that he understood and then pushed back on a big steel lever.

Instantly, a thick mass of cement began pouring down the slide hanging from the truck's storage cylinder. All the kids pushed forward to watch. The cement dropped twenty feet down into the trench that had been dug for it.

When the trench was completely filled, it would be the foundation for the new bank building. But all the cement was not going to be poured that day. The foreman had told Billy it would take more than thirty cement mixers full of cement to fill the trench. That was all right with Billy and his friends. They felt as if they could watch the big trucks pour cement for the rest of the year and not get tired of it.

After the first truck was empty, the kids watched the second being moved into place. They watched it empty out into the trench below. Then they watched it be replaced by a third. And a fourth, and a fifth, and a sixth.

By the time the seventh cement mixer was being moved up, Malcomb said, "Hey, it's six o'clock already." He grabbed his book bag up off the ground and slipped it over his shoulders, saying, "I got to get home."

"Yeah," agreed Mike reluctantly. "Me, too."

All the boys decided they had better leave, including Billy. His dad had said he would try to make it that night, but he couldn't promise he would be there. He said it was possible that he might have to see a late patient. If he did, he wouldn't be able to pick them up. Since most of the other kids had left for home already, Billy decided he'd better not wait any longer.

On the way home, the guys talked about the usual things—what was on TV that night, how the local baseball team's chances were shaping up. Then Malcomb brought up something none of them had ever talked about before.

"Hey," he asked, already knowing what Billy thought, "did any of you guys feel anything funny this morning?"

"Funny?" asked Jack. "What are you talking about?"

"Yeah," added Mike. "You mean 'funny-ha-ha' or 'funny-strange'?"

"Funny-strange," answered Malcomb. "When we were coming into the school. Did any of you guys think anything was weird?"

Malcomb acted like he was asking everyone, but he stared right at Billy. Billy knew the heavyset boy was waiting for him to say something. He wished someone else would say something first. Especially Danny. Billy did not feel like being on the firing end of his friend's jokes just then. Not about this, anyway.

Danny did not say anything, however. Nor did Jack or Mike. So reluctantly Billy said, "I did."

"Weird?" Danny asked. "Like what?"

"I don't know," answered Billy. Malcomb shrugged his shoulders, not knowing what he could add.

"If you don't know," asked Danny, "then how do you know it was weird?"

All the boys had stopped on the corner. It was the point where they had to split up—Jack, Mike, and Malcomb going left, Danny and Billy going right. As everyone stared at him, waiting for him to say something else, Billy said, "It was just strange, is all. I . . . I thought I felt the side-walk—I don't know—move."

"Yeah," agreed Malcomb. "Like it moved, or like there was an electric shock running through it."

"Concrete doesn't conduct electricity, tubby," Danny sneered.

"I *know* that," answered Malcomb. "I said it was *like* there was a shock. I don't know what else to call it."

"I do."

All the boys turned back to look at Billy again. None of them said anything. Something in his tone warned them that what he was about to say was very serious.

"You know that feeling you get when you're all alone—say in a dark house at night? Maybe you've been reading a monster story, or watching something scary on TV?"

His four friends all nodded their heads.

"And you know that there's no reason to be scared, but you're still scared anyway? It's like when you know that if any little thing were to happen—even just a noise you weren't ex-pecting—that you'd jump right out of your skin?"

Mike and Jack stared at Billy, feeling a little confused. Malcomb kept on nodding. He knew ex-actly what Billy meant. Danny stood with his arms folded across his chest, not saying anything. Not caring, Billy kept talking. "Well, that's how I felt this morning when we came into the school-yard. Just for a minute—a second, really—it was like there was a pair of creepy eyes watching me . . . studying everything I did."

"That's it," mumbled Malcomb. The heavyset boy did not even realize he was talking.

As Jack and Mike turned to look at Malcomb,

Billy added, "Except that it didn't feel as if there wasn't anything to be scared about."

"What?" asked Danny.

"It felt like there was plenty to be scared about."

"Awww," said Mike, "you're putting us on."

"No, he's not," said Malcomb. "That's just what I felt. That's just what I felt."

"Ahh, who cares what you felt, butterball?" asked Jack. He pushed the heavy boy, adding, "You two just made this stuff up to goof on us."

Billy started to protest, but Danny interrupted. Taking a single step forward, he said, "No. They didn't." Then he stared at his best friend, asking him, "Did you?"

"Uh-uh," said Billy, shaking his head. "I know this sounds goofy. It all happened so fast I didn't even think about it until after we were in homeroom. It's just a . . . a *feeling,* really, that's sort of been bugging me all day."

Billy was glad he had backed Malcomb up. He had not realized how greatly he had been disturbed by the moment in front of the school that morning until he had started to talk about it. Now that he had, he realized that for just a split second, he had been really—*really*—scared. But, he asked himself, of what? What could I have been scared of?

"You guys are nuts," said Mike. "Come on, Jack. Even doing homework is better than listening to this."

As the two boys took off, Malcomb said, "I believe you, Billy. I felt it, too. I don't know what it was. But there was something there, all right. Something I hope I never meet."

Then Malcomb noticed that Mike and Jack were half a block down the street. He didn't want them to make fun of him, but he also didn't want to walk home alone. Turning away, he started to run after the other two boys, yelling back to Billy and Danny, "I'll see you guys on Monday." Then he chased Mike and Jack down the street.

Billy and Danny watched him for a moment. Then they started off in the other direction toward their own homes. Neither one of them mentioned the conversation the five of them had just had. Neither one of them knew what to say. But it was too late for silence. The thing under the grass had already heard all it needed to hear.

So, it thought, *he knows.*

4

He knows.

The thing lay beneath the ground, wondering what it should do next. For the first time in all its existence, it was not certain.

He knows.

It had traveled the stars for almost a billion years. Always it had followed the same pattern. Whenever it reached a new world, it first buried itself beneath the surface. Then it would reach upward through cracks in the ground . . . looking for souls.

It would steal the souls from the creatures it could catch—one by one—growing stronger with each feasting.

In the beginning, it always had to move slowly. Its first few feedings usually took a long time to arrange. Moving from planet to planet took a lot of its energy.

Whenever it arrived on a new world, it always came hungry. But it also arrived very weak from its journey.

How? it wondered. *How does he know?*

Each new victim supplied it with a great deal of energy. After a while, it could move through the ground quickly, catching dozens at a time.

After a while. But not at first. Not now.

This world is different. I must proceed with caution.

Never before had the thing beneath the grass encountered a planet quite like Earth. It was not used to dealing with thinking creatures. Most of the worlds it had found—which it had invaded and destroyed—had been populated with animals of limited intelligence.

I must not make any more mistakes.

Of course, it had found civilized planets before. Early in its life, it had come across quite a number of them. But it had been a much more careful hunter then. And that had been a long time ago.

Since that time, all the worlds it encountered had been easy to strip of their life. The thing beneath the ground had gotten overconfident.

Careless. I have been too careless.

It snarled at itself, remembering the chief of the Taranka tribe. The old Indian had tricked it. He had drawn the monster away from the rest of the tribe. The chief had sacrificed himself so his people could live, not realizing he had saved all the humans of his time by doing so.

By the time the creature hidden under the ground had turned to strike at the rest of the tribe, it found that they had run too far for it to catch them. It had just arrived on this world then. It had not thought the Indians would be any trouble for it. It had been wrong.

I must not be careless this time.

For centuries after the death of their chief, the Tarankans warned everyone to stay away from the valley. By keeping people away, the Indians kept the monster hungry and turned the valley into its prison. They killed all the animals that tried to enter the area as well.

For over six hundred years they kept the thing beneath the grass at bay—starving it slowly.

Then the white man came.

The Tarankans warned them that a terrible monster lived beneath the ground in the valley. The explorers did not believe them. A small war was fought, and although they fought bravely, all the Tarankans were killed.

After that, the white settlers began to move into the valley. They encountered no monster. No souls were stolen, no people were torn apart— which only made the settlers laugh at the Indians they had killed. But . . .

The monster was still there.

It was only sleeping.

I must be careful.

The Taranka tribe had starved the thing beneath the grass for so long, it had fallen into a deep sleep. In fact, if only a few hundred more years had passed, it would have died. But . . .

That did not happen.

Instead, a settlement was build directly above it. A settlement that grew into a village. A village that grew into a town. A town that grew into a city. The city of Darbenburg, population 27,439.

The city where Billy Carne lived.

Very careful.

5

Friday evening, after supper, Billy was waiting in Danny's backyard. Danny had gone inside a few minutes earlier. He had wanted to see if there was any cold soda or juice in the house. Billy and he had played catch for an hour. Now they were both hot and sweaty. And very thirsty.

Once Danny had gone inside, however, he had not made it back outside. Billy had heard his friend's mother shouting at him to do his chores. Danny had stuck his head back out the door and whispered, "It will only take me a minute. Honest. Hang out. Don't go anywhere."

"Sure," Billy had told him.

After that, Danny had disappeared back inside. Billy threw himself into the big wooden chair Danny's father always sat in when he was in the backyard. Then Billy settled back to wait.

At first he planned out when he would get his weekend homework done. The teachers had really, *really* piled it on. But before Billy realized it, he was thinking again about what had happened that morning.

He thought about what Malcomb had said. He thought about what he had felt. Then he closed his eyes, trying to remember exactly what it felt like.

He could remember the moment clearly. He could remember all of them walking on Munsen. But they were still outside school property then. That wasn't when it happened.

He could remember them entering the schoolyard. He could see them in his head, could remember every word they said as they came up the walk.

No, he told himself, we weren't talking on the walk. The bell had rung. We were running.

Running up the walk when it happened.

When what happened? he asked himself. What? What is this terrible thing that happened?

Billy forced himself to think. Keeping his eyes squeezed shut, he tried to remember what was so different about coming into school that morning.

Different from all the other thousands of mornings he had passed through the same gate . . .

had walked up the same walk . . . had gone into the same school.

"What?" he said out loud. "What was so different?"

The smell.

He heard the words in his head. He repeated them out loud slowly. First he said them like a question.

"The smell?"

And then he remembered.

"The smell!" he said again.

Like burning air, like burning wires inside a radio or TV. That electrical smell. I remember. It was just a whiff. Just a tiny whiff . . . but I remember.

The morning came back to him inside his head. He could see it all in slow motion. They were half-way up the walk when he had caught the smell in the air. But they were moving too fast to pay any attention. They had to get into the school.

But, now that he thought about it, he could remember the smell. And it was just a second after that when he felt the sidewalk shake.

"And . . . and the grass."

Yes! The grass on both sides of the sidewalk had moved. He could remember hearing it move.

41

There was no wind, and yet he had heard the grass move.

The grass had moved, and the sidewalk had moved. He could see it in his head—the pebbles dancing, the cement chipping where the sections of sidewalk met.

"Yeah," he whispered. "And that was when I felt like something was watching us."

Billy looked at Danny's house. He wondered how much longer his friend would be. He wanted to ask Danny if he remembered any of the things Billy had recalled.

Did Danny remember it the way he did? Did he remember how the sidewalk moved? Had he seen the little pieces of rock bouncing around?

Had he heard the grass moving?

And the smell?

Especially the smell.

"He *has* to remember that."

Billy bolted up out of the big wooden chair. He was too excited to keep sitting. He actually had something that Danny might remember.

"Nobody in the world could forget that weird odor. He *has* to remember that."

Billy tried to think of a way to describe the smell. He couldn't just ask Danny if he remembered a weird smell. He had to be able to describe it.

It was a burning smell. That much he was sure of. But burning what? Burning wire, burning rubber, or something electrical. It wasn't a natural smell—like burning wood, or leaves, or anything like that.

This was a smell like when his family's washing machine had broken, and the basement had been full of smoke. Just that kind of smell.

"Yeah," he said out loud, pleased with himself for having remembered the perfect example. "Just like that."

Just like that smell I smell right now, he thought.

And then Billy realized what he was telling himself. His head jerked around. First left, then right.

He could smell it again.

He *could!*

And then he realized that all around him the grass in Danny's yard was starting to shake.

And that beneath his feet the cement of Danny's back porch was beginning to vibrate.

Before he knew it, Billy was screaming as loud as he could.

6

"Billy!" shouted Danny's father. He ran out of the house as fast as he could, jumping down the stairs. "What's the matter? What are you screaming about?"

"Danny!" Billy screamed. "It was here!"

"What?" asked Danny. "What was here?"

"The same thing from this morning at school. It was here in your yard!"

"What thing?" demanded Mr. Hawkes. "What are you talking about?"

Billy squirmed as Mr. Hawkes held on to him. By that time, everyone in the house had come out to the backyard. Danny and his mother and father. His older sister and her girlfriend. Even the dog.

Neighbors on both sides of Danny's house had heard him as well. People were stepping out onto

44

their porches. Looking out their doors and windows.

Everyone was staring.

Staring at Billy.

"It was . . . it was a . . . a . . . a . . ."

A what? Billy thought. What was it?

Suddenly, Billy realized the situation he was in. He had started screaming as soon as he had smelled the burning air. Screaming really loud. Everyone had come running to see what was the matter.

What do I tell them? he thought. Looking around the quiet backyard, he wondered, What *can* I tell them?

Hoping that Danny would remember what he had, he turned to his friend. "Danny, do you remember what Malcomb and I were talking about before?"

"Yeah . . . ?"

"This morning—do you remember when we were coming into school. Do you remember what happened?"

"You mean what you and Malcomb said? About a creepy feeling and all?"

"No, no—I mean, do you remember it happening?" When his friend just stared at him, Billy asked, "Do you remember the smell?"

45

"What smell?"

"That burning smell? Like from a hot television set. Don't you remember it?"

Danny tried hard to think. Everyone was staring right at him. His whole family. His sister's creepy friend. Even all of his neighbors. Only the dog had walked off to investigate something in the back corner of the yard. Everyone else was still staring.

Danny wanted to help Billy, but everyone was looking at him, and he didn't know what to say.

"Danny," Mr. Hawkes interrupted. "What's going on? What is Billy talking about?"

Danny turned toward his father. Mr. Hawkes looked angry. He was still holding on to Billy. Billy was still squirming and kicking, trying to get away from him. Danny did not know what to say . . . what to do.

He had started to think that he remembered a little of what Billy and Malcomb had been talking about. But what was he supposed to do? What?

Tell his father they had all had a creepy feeling in front of the school, and that was why Billy was screaming now in their backyard?

No way.

Mr. Hawkes did not like silly games or foolishness. That kind of thing just made him mad. And no matter what Danny could think of to say, he was sure his father would think he was just being goofy.

Afraid to make his father even angrier than he already was, Danny told him, "I . . . I don't know, Dad."

"Hey, Frank," called out one of Danny's neighbors to his father. "Everything all right over there?"

"I don't know, George," Danny's father answered the man. "That's what I'm trying to find out."

Mr. Hawkes turned Billy around so they were facing each other. Looking Billy straight in the eye, he told him in a deep, angry voice, "Now, young man—you just settle down and tell me what this is all about."

Billy stopped squirming. He was close to crying. And he was really, really frightened. But the horrible thing was, he didn't know what he was so frightened of. He didn't know what to do.

The same thing that had happened that morning in front of the school had happened again there in Danny's yard. But, he thought, how to prove it? He didn't see any way he could possibly do that. To tell the truth, he didn't even know what he was trying to prove.

Looking over at his friend, he asked him in a pleading voice, "Danny, can't you smell it? In the air—here—right now? Can't you?"

"Smell what, Billy? *What?*"

Billy looked first to the left. Then to the right. Mr. Hawkes still looked real angry. Mrs. Hawkes seemed worried. Danny's sister and her friend just looked bored. Nobody looked very happy.

He turned his head in every direction, trying to see which of Danny's neighbors were still staring at him. Most of them were, but some had already gone back into their houses. He could hear their doors closing and their windows shutting.

"What was it, Billy?" Danny asked again. "Just tell us what it was."

I wish I knew, he thought.

Billy was starting to feel very foolish. What was he supposed to tell everyone?

That he had gotten so scared . . . that he was ready to cry . . . because he heard the grass moving?

Because he felt the ground tremble?

Because he smelled something burning?

Looking Mr. Hawkes in the eye, afraid to say anything else, Billy answered, "It was nothing."

Danny's father let Billy go. Standing up

48

straight, Mr. Hawkes asked, "All of this? The screaming and the carrying on, and all this talk about bad smells—all of it was just *nothing?*"

"Yes, sir," Billy mumbled.

"So what was it, Frank?" shouted Mr. Hawkes's neighbor.

"Just a friend of Danny's . . . forgot that April Fool's Day was last month."

Billy bit at his lip as he heard more of Danny's neighbors going back inside. He could hear them mumbling.

"Crazy kid."

"Little goof."

"What's the matter with children these days?"

"Someone should tell his parents."

Billy did not know what to do. He wanted to just run away. But he knew he couldn't do that. That was something a little kid would do. Knowing he had to say something before Mr. Hawkes got mad again, he said, "I'm sorry. I . . . I just thought I smelled something really bad, and then heard something . . . and . . . I guess I just scared myself."

Danny's sister and her friend went back into the house. His mother followed them, shaking her head sadly. The three of them whispered to one another. Then they all laughed as they went inside.

Mr. Hawkes didn't laugh, however. Stepping forward toward his son, he said, "Danny, I think you'd better get inside and get started on your homework."

"Yes, sir," said Danny. He wanted to say goodbye to Billy—to talk to him for just a second—but he didn't dare. His father was too angry. He'd have to wait and call Billy later.

Turning to Billy, Mr. Hawkes said, "And I think you'd better get yourself home, young man."

"Yes, sir," answered Billy.

Hanging his head, he went over to the table on the porch to get his glove. After stuffing it back into his schoolbag, he slid his bag onto his shoulders. Then he turned back around just in time to see the rear door to Danny's house closing.

Great, he thought. Just great. Now everybody thinks I'm crazy.

Walking down Danny's driveway, Billy wondered if maybe he wasn't going a little crazy.

He had been scaring himself all day. He couldn't even say what he'd been scaring himself with because he didn't know.

Yes. He did.

A smell.

He'd been scaring himself over a smell.

Billy felt like an idiot. When he got to the end of Danny's driveway, he turned and looked back at the house. In a whisper, he said, "I've been acting like a jerk. Even if I *did* smell something and hear it and all—so what? So what? It was just a smell and the grass moving. Big deal."

Billy started to walk toward home.

"It's not like anyone got hurt or anything."

As he walked, he wondered how long it would take his parents to find out about what had happened. He also wondered what they would do to him.

Unfortunately, he should have been wondering about other things.

Like what had happened to Danny's dog.

If he had, he might have saved a lot of people a lot of trouble.

A *lot* of trouble.

7

The next day would be the worst Saturday morning of Billy's life. The absolute worst. As it went on—hour after hour—he discovered that everybody in town knew about what he had done the night before at Danny's house.

Including his parents.

Billy found them in the kitchen. His mother was making breakfast. His father was reading a magazine. At first Billy didn't realize that they knew anything about what had happened the night before.

He found out soon enough, though.

His father was the first to bring it up.

"So," Dr. Carne said, pretending not to be concerned, "tell me about all this commotion last night."

"Last night?" asked Billy. He hoped his father

was referring to something else. He wasn't, however. Billy felt his heart stop as Dr. Carne said, "Yes—over at Danny's house. Wasn't it, dear?"

"Yes, Charles," answered Billy's mother without turning back from the stove. Normally she would have turned around to answer her husband, but that wasn't part of the *plan*.

And Billy's parents always followed their *plan*. The night before when they first heard about what had happened from one of Danny's neighbors, they had sat down to make a plan. They discussed a few different ways to handle things, but finally agreed not to talk about it that night.

First, they would let Billy get some sleep. They could wait. They would all sleep and then ask him about what had happened in the morning.

Dr. and Mrs. Carne had agreed that Dr. Carne would handle the questioning. That he would sit at the table with his magazine and that Mrs. Carne would make pancakes.

They chose pancakes because that was Billy's favorite breakfast. They didn't want to upset him. They wanted him to feel relaxed. They just wanted to help.

The problem was, of course, that neither Dr. nor Mrs. Carne had the slightest idea of what the real

53

problem was. They just figured that Billy was going through some crazy phase or something.

And Billy knew it.

He was wise to the way his parents worked. He knew they were concerned. He knew they wanted to help. He also knew that if he told them anything about what really happened, they would never believe him in a zillion years.

Oh, sure, they would believe that Billy believed what he was saying.

They were good parents, and they loved their son. But Billy's father was a psychiatrist and his mother was a lawyer. His parents just weren't the kind of people who believed in anything they couldn't see.

And, thought Billy, even I haven't actually *seen* anything yet. I've smelled something, and heard something, and even *felt* something. But ... I haven't *seen* anything.

"So, anyway," continued Dr. Carne, carefully not looking up from his magazine so he wouldn't appear too interested, "what was all that about last night?"

Hoping for the best, Billy played the game with his father. Reaching for the syrup, he said, "Oh, nothing."

"Nothing?" asked Dr. Carne, not ready to let

the matter go yet. "We heard that you seemed very upset. We called Danny's parents, and that's what his father told us—didn't he, dear?"

"That was Danny's mother, actually."

"Oh, oh. Right. That's right. So, it was 'nothing.' What kind of 'nothing'?"

"Oh, you know," Billy answered while putting some syrup on his pancakes. "Just . . . well . . . I just thought I heard something scary. I thought I smelled something burning . . . and . . . and . . . I just got scared for a minute."

Billy took a bite of his pancakes. He didn't want his father to make a big deal out of this. He knew he would sound like an idiot if he tried to explain what he was really feeling.

To tell the truth, he was hoping that he could just forget about it.

"But you're not scared now?" asked his father.

"Nah," Billy answered, taking another bite. "I feel kind of stupid for getting everybody upset and all. But that's about it."

"Are you sure?"

Billy realized his father wasn't quite convinced. Trying to sound as relaxed as possible, he said, "Oh, yeah. I mean, what's there to be scared of?"

Billy worked on his pancakes. Peeking out of the corner of his eye, he saw his father and mother give each other a secret look. They were checking with each other to see if they agreed that everything was all right. When his father changed the subject, Billy figured they were satisfied.

Good, he thought. Now that that's over, everything can get back to normal.

But then Billy found out just how many people had heard about his screaming.

Before breakfast was over, his aunt and a cousin called. Both of them had heard and wanted to know what had happened. He could tell from the way his mother lowered her voice and then walked out of the room with the phone both times.

Both the mail and the morning paper came before he could leave the house. Both the mailman and the paperboy gave Billy strange looks.

After he left the house, it only got worse. It seemed to him that everyone was looking at him. From over their fences. From their doors and windows. Even from their cars as they drove past him.

Good grief, he thought, it's like the whole town knows already. Don't people have anything better to do around here than gossip about something stupid like this?

Billy wasn't actually certain that everyone was looking at him. But it sure seemed as if they were. Several people—some adults and some kids—stopped him while he was walking to ask him about the night before. It was enough to make him wish he hadn't left the house.

Only, if I'd stayed home, he thought, I'd just have had to listen to the phone all day, and Mom telling everyone I'm not crazy.

Billy kicked a rock on the sidewalk, sending it flying out into the street. He had planned to go to the school ball field. A bunch of the guys were getting up a practice game and he needed all the fielding practice he could get.

But, he thought, what's the point? I don't want to go there if everyone's going to keep staring at me like I'm from Jupiter or something.

Billy hesitated for a moment, then he said out loud, "I don't need people thinking I'm crazy."

And then he suddenly saw a problem he had not thought of before. Did he hear and feel and smell something—twice—or didn't he? If he didn't, then maybe he *was* crazy. If he did, then what the heck was it?

Billy stopped walking.

What could he do?

What?

If he tried to tell anyone about what had happened, they might put him away. His father was a psychiatrist. He knew that when people got an idea into their head that they couldn't prove, the police and the doctors and everyone sometimes put them in a hospital for their own good.

But, he thought, I know I really did feel something watching me. Something bad. Something . . .

Evil.

As silly as he felt using the word, he knew it was the right one. It *had* been something evil. Something evil had watched him and his friends as they went into the school. Something evil had come after him in Danny's backyard.

It had.

And he knew it.

"So if I tell anyone, they'll lock me up for being crazy. But if I don't tell anyone . . ."

What? He wondered for a moment, *What* would happen if he didn't tell anyone? Somehow, he knew the thing that had been watching him had been evil. He knew it meant him harm.

In fact, the more he thought about it, the more convinced he became that, whatever the thing was that had been watching him, it meant a lot of people harm.

It meant everybody harm.

Everybody in the world.

"But," he said out loud, "what can I *do* about it?"

"About what?"

Billy spun around. His eyes bulged. There, standing right behind him, was Mr. Knisbaum.

"About what, Carne?"

"What . . . what do you mean, sir?"

"Hey, don't try to dodge your way around me." Mr. Knisbaum took a step toward Billy. He was the tallest, heaviest teacher in the school. He was a huge man—the biggest man in town. Between that and his long hair and curly, wild beard, every kid in school was afraid of him. As his shadow fell over Billy, the teacher said, "So, like I said before . . . 'About what?' What is it that's got you all tied up in knots?"

Billy was afraid now. No one ever knew what Mr. Knisbaum was going to do. He was strict and tough and never let anyone get away with anything.

But, Billy thought suddenly, he's always fair. Nobody's ever said he wasn't.

Billy looked up at the big teacher. He needed to talk to someone. He knew he couldn't talk to his parents. He knew he couldn't talk to his friends. Malcomb agreed with him, but was afraid to admit it. Mike and Jack didn't agree and weren't afraid to say so.

Danny probably thought he was crazy.

Hey, he thought, maybe I am. But I'm not going to find out if I keep hiding from whatever's wrong.

And then Danny told Mr. Knisbaum everything.

That went well.

The thing beneath the grass chuckled to itself. It was still resting after having terrorized Billy the night before. But it couldn't stop thinking about what it had done.

It was pleased with itself for being so clever.

Soon it would be rested. Then it could go out and start looking for more victims. Like that tasty little dog.

A few more like that, and it would be rested and covered in blood and filled with energy.

Just because it was so clever.

Must get ready. Before long it will be time for the hunt to begin.

The monster had watched the boys walking to school. It didn't know what a school was, and it didn't care. It was just hungry and wanted some-thing to eat. It wanted a soul.

But it noticed something about Billy. Some-thing that made it want to move slowly.

Carefully.

The chief of the Tarankans had been too clever for it. He had died so his people could escape. The creature had captured his soul, and a handful of others. But it did not get enough energy from those killings to leave the valley it had landed in. And the surviving Tarankans had made cer-tain that it got no more.

The leader tricked me that time. Not this time, though. This time, I will trick the leader.

When the monster had watched Billy and his friends, it had seen easily that Billy was the leader of his group. Using its powers, it had sent a piece of its mind into Billy's. First, it wanted to learn about how the world had changed while it had been asleep.

Second, it wanted to learn about the new leader it saw walking down the street with his followers. It learned everything it needed to know. It found out what a school was. It learned about the changes in the world since it had first arrived on the Earth.

The thing beneath the grass learned about

62

telephones and television. It learned that if it was not careful, the people living in its new hunting ground could tell one another about it quickly.

Then they might hunt it, instead of the other way around. The thing beneath the grass did not want that to happen.

It didn't want that at all.

So it decided to scare the new leader it had found. As a test. First it would scare him. Then it would scare him again. And again. Until no one trusted him anymore.

The thing knew that no one would follow a leader that they didn't trust.

So, it thought, all it had to do was make certain that no one trusted Billy. The monster had made a mistake in letting the boy sense its presence. But, now that it had, it would correct its mistake.

It would scare him and make him seem like a fool until no one cared about him anymore.

The creature that had sucked dry a million worlds was very sure that this time, it would win.

Very sure, indeed.

In fact, it felt it could taste Billy's soul already.

"Well," said Mr. Knisbaum, "I have to admit that that's quite a story."

"Yeah," agreed Billy. "But what do I do with it?"

"Good question," answered the teacher. "What do you want to do with it?"

"What do you mean?"

"I mean," asked Mr. Knisbaum, "what do you want to do next?"

Billy hadn't thought about that. As he did, the teacher asked him, "Do you want to find out more about this, or do you just want to forget it?"

"But . . ."

Billy did not know what to say. Sure, he wanted to find out more—find some proof he could show people. But how? Where could he find something like that?

64

"But what, Carne?"

"Mr. Knisbaum," he finally managed to say. "Yeah. I want to find out more. Sure I do. I don't want people thinking I'm crazy. But where . . . I mean, how? I mean . . ."

The big man held up his hand. Billy stopped talking. Mr. Knisbaum told him, "When you want to know what something is—when you want to know *anything*—what do you do?"

Billy thought for a long moment. Then, when he felt he had the answer, he asked, "Look it up?"

"Give the man an A," answered Mr. Knisbaum. "Now, why don't you go for the A-plus. Tell me, *where* would you go to look something like this up?"

Billy thought again, then said, "The library."

"A-plus work, Carne."

Of course, thought Billy. Of course, I can look it up in the library. But *where?*

Catching the suddenly worried look on Billy's face, Mr. Knisbaum asked, "What's the matter, Carne?"

"It's not that I don't think you have a good idea, Mr. Knisbaum," Billy told the teacher. "You do. It's a great idea—it's perfect. It's just that . . . well, I . . ."

"You don't know where to look—right?"

65

Billy nodded his head. Mr. Knisbaum put his lips tight together. Billy could see that he was thinking about something. He couldn't imagine what, though.

Finally, the teacher stopped thinking and said, "You're probably thinking that I would know where to look—aren't you?"

Billy nodded again.

Mr. Knisbaum sighed, then said, "You know, you're probably right."

Billy suddenly felt as if a big weight had been pulled off his chest. He had been scared to tell anyone the truth about what had been going on.

Terrified.

But to tell Mr. Knisbaum—Mr. *Knisbaum*—that was scarier than telling his parents.

Ten times scarier.

But now he was very glad he had told him. Before he could say "Thank you" or anything at all, the teacher started to walk back in the other direction. As he did, he shouted, "Come on, Carne. I'll go with you to the library. I'll help you find some books. But I'm not doing the work for you. You'll have to read them yourself."

Billy ran and caught up with Mr. Knisbaum right away. For the first time that day, things were finally looking up.

*   *   *

"Excuse me, son . . . I just wanted to check and see if you found everything you were looking for?"

Billy looked up at the librarian. He was surprised at what the woman told him. She had mentioned earlier that she would come back in an hour to see how he was doing. That meant he had spent almost the entire afternoon in the library.

Who cares? he thought. It was worth it.

Billy thanked the librarian for checking on him. He told her that he had found just what he needed, and that he was just about to leave. As she went away, he grabbed up all the books he and Mr. Knisbaum had pulled from the shelves. Then he headed for the front of the library.

He put some of the books into the box the library left out for books people did not want. That was where he put the two books on fire and wind he and Mr. Knisbaum had decided he should try.

He hadn't found anything in the book on wind about it making noises like the ones he had heard. Or anything about grass moving without the wind blowing. Or anything useful.

The same with the book on fire. Nothing on people smelling things like he had smelled. Or

67

burning smells appearing where there was no fire. Nothing.

He put in the book on monsters and the book on superstitions. He had looked through them both. But they hadn't had anything for him, either.

But the book on the history of Darbenburg— that he checked out. That had something for him.

Something important.

"Okay," said Danny. "So, we're all here. So what was so important?"

Billy stared at Danny. He wondered why his friend was so mad at him.

Maybe, he thought, his dad yelled at him last night after I went home.

Mike and Jack didn't seem as if they were very happy with him, either. Even Malcomb looked unhappy about being there. Not knowing what else to do, Billy asked, "Hey guys, what's the matter?"

At first, none of his friends would say anything. Malcomb looked off up into the sky. Danny kept shaking his head. Jack and Mike didn't even sit. They both just stood next to each other with their hands on their hips. Then suddenly, Mike spoke up.

"The matter is," he said in a harsh voice, "you called all of us and told us to come over right away. I don't know about these other guys, but my mom heard about what you did at Danny's last night, and she doesn't want me hanging around with you anymore."

"Mine, too," said Jack. "She thinks you're nuts."

"Awww, your mom thinks everyone's nuts," Mike cut in. At first he made Billy feel better, but then he added, "But my mom told my dad about it, and when I told him you were okay, he started yelling at me."

Danny looked at his friend for a minute without saying anything. Finally, however, he admitted, "It's the same for everybody. You creeped everyone out last night. So come on, already. What's so important you had us all sneak over here?"

Billy held up the book on the history of Darbenburg and said, "This." Then, before any of the boys could say anything, he told them. "What happened last night—what we were talking about yesterday after school . . . it's all happened before."

While everyone looked at him, Billy opened the book to a place he had marked earlier. As he found the spot he wanted, he told the other boys, "The guy that wrote this book found out everything he could about the whole town . . . including stuff that happened even before there was a town. One of the things he put in was this old Indian legend. Now, you listen to this."

Billy opened the book wide and began to read.

" 'The main reason the town was settled so much later than the rest of the state was that the vast Darbenburg valley was considered cursed by the Taranka Indians. This now-vanished tribe not only shunned the area, but actually made war on those who tried to enter it.' "

Billy peeked at his friends. Malcomb was fascinated. Mike and Jack looked as if they were interested, but were pretending hard not to be. Danny looked pretty interested. Feeling more confident, Billy kept reading.

" 'The Tarankans claimed that a monster lived under the ground in the valley. They called it Redmawnachu—the soul stealer. Supposedly, the soul stealer waited for people to step on cracks in the earth, and then would suck their souls out of their bodies down into the ground.' "

Billy took a deep breath. The most important part of what he had found was in the last paragraph.

" 'The legend said that Redmawnachu shook the ground as it moved beneath it. Supposedly, there were two ways one might spot the soul stealer. The first was in the movement of the ground. On windless days, the Indians claimed to be able to see the grass moving above it as it traveled beneath the ground. The second was a foul, burning odor that was said to accompany the arrival of Redmawnachu.' "

Billy shut the book. Looking around at the others, he asked, "Well?"

"Well, what?" asked Danny.

"Well, what? Well, don't you see what's going on?"

"No, I don't." Danny sat back in his lawn chair. Folding his arms across his chest, he said, "I don't see what that's got to do with anything."

"The burning smell? The grass moving without any wind? Yesterday in front of the school . . . last night at your place . . . it was the same thing both times."

All the boys looked at Billy as if he were strange.

Even Malcomb.

Even Danny.

"It said that the Indians were wiped out because they kept fighting anybody that wanted to enter the valley. They felt that if they kept people away from this thing, it would get weak and die."

"Yeah, that's what they thought," admitted Mike. "But they all got killed and Darbenburg got built, and there ain't never been no soul stealer running around town."

"Oh, but there is now." Jack laughed. "The Indians' bogeyman has come back to make Billy wet his pants."

Mike laughed. Danny chuckled. As Billy stayed in his chair, feeling helpless, Jack and Mike jumped up. Heading for the driveway, Mike said, "I'm out of here. You *are* nuts, Carne."

Billy watched them leaving, not knowing what to do. Then, before he could do anything, Malcomb got up to follow them.

"Malcomb," cried Billy. "Not you, too."

"I got to go," he said. The heavyset boy did not look Billy in the eye. Billy got up out of his chair. He grabbed Malcomb's arm and said, "You felt it. You said you did. You know I'm not crazy. *You* know if anyone does."

Frightened—and ashamed of being so frightened—Malcomb said, "Look, we were just . . . I don't know . . . scaring ourselves yesterday. But this . . ." Malcomb pointed toward the history book in Billy's hand. "This stuff . . . you're acting nutty, Billy. Like you're trying to turn this into some kind of horror movie or something."

As Billy stood by quietly, Malcomb ran down the driveway. As the heavyset boy disappeared from sight, Billy turned to Danny and told him, "He's scared. That's all. He's just scared. But I don't get it. I mean, we should be sticking together."

"Sticking together?" asked Danny. "Why? What for?"

"What for?" Billy repeated. "Are you kidding me? Are you nuts? That *thing* is out there somewhere."

Danny shook his head. Walking toward the driveway, he told his friend, "Billy—you're talking crazy. There's no *thing* out there, or anywhere. Get real, man. You read this stuff and all of a sudden you think you're a ghostbuster, or something."

"But, Danny . . ."

"No, you shut up." Danny backed away from his friend as if he was more frightened of him than of anything else. "You think you've caught on to some big secret and it's got you acting crazy."

Turning away from his friend, Danny walked down the driveway, saying, "I've got better things

73

to do than listen to you. I've got to go look for my dog. Your crazy act must have scared him off because no one's seen him since last night."

Danny kept walking. Then he stopped and turned around at the end of the driveway. Looking back at his friend, he called out to him, "You'd better have a long talk with your dad. Because I think you really *need* a shrink, Billy."

Billy put the history book down on the patio table. It was supposed to prove that he wasn't imagining things. It was supposed to change things for him.

It changed things, all right, he thought bitterly. It changed everything.

Billy fought back the tears he could feel building behind his eyes. He had been so sure that the book would convince his friends. But now it had turned them all against him.

Now he had no friends.

He didn't have anything except the certain knowledge that there was a monster living under Darbenburg. And that he could do nothing to stop it.

Nothing at all.

Billy felt very cold. Even though it was the middle of May. Even though there was no wind.

Suddenly he was alone and feeling very cold. And frightened.

Very frightened.

And, out in the yard, under the grass, the destroyer of a million worlds smiled to itself as it thought, *Now . . . now the hunt begins.*

10

Billy walked down the driveway, watching the other boys disappear off in the distance. He stopped at the point where the driveway met the sidewalk. Then he just stared.

Why won't they believe me?

Billy wondered about what had gone wrong for a long time. He had found proof that he wasn't crazy. They should have listened to him.

They should have.

I would have listened if I were one of them.

Then the same cold feeling that had been bothering Billy a minute earlier returned. It made him shiver. He rubbed his arms to try and make them feel warmer.

Then suddenly he felt stupid, standing at the end of the driveway just staring out into space.

What am I going to do? he wondered. I can't just stand here staring forever.

People already thought Billy was getting strange enough. He knew he couldn't afford to let them see him doing anything else strange. He looked down at the history book in his hands. It was supposed to have convinced his friends that something horrible was happening. It was supposed to have fixed everything.

It hadn't. It hadn't convinced any of his friends of anything, except that he was crazy.

Now Billy Carne knew he had no friends. He was totally alone. Alone with the book about the history of Darbenburg that had lost him all his friends.

"Well," he said out loud, staring at the book, "no sense keeping you. Might as well just take you back to the library and get rid of you."

Billy knew it would be at least an hour until dinnertime. Knowing no one would be looking for him until then, he decided to take the history book back right then and there.

Moving out onto the sidewalk, Billy headed for the library. He walked slowly. He was in no hurry. Why should he be? What was the point of hurrying?

I go to the library, he thought, I come back. I

eat dinner, I go to bed. I get up in the morning and then I just do it all over again.

Billy kicked a pebble out of his way. It shot forward and rolled out into the street.

I wait for that thing to come and get me . . . me and everybody else.

Billy kicked another stone off the sidewalk out into the road. As it bounced between two parked cars, he said, "I wonder where that thing is, anyway?"

Billy kicked another pebble. It rolled for the street just like the others, but didn't quite make it off the sidewalk. Billy stared at it, saying, "Great. Now I can't even kick rocks right."

Walking over toward the edge of the sidewalk, Billy went to kick the little stone again. He was mad at it for not making it into the street.

Well, he thought, it'll get there this time. I'll kick it so hard it'll get to the moon.

Billy pulled his leg back to kick. And then, just before he swung his leg, he noticed something. The pebble he had kicked last . . . it had come to a stop in a crack in the sidewalk.

In a crack.

Billy's eyes fixed on the crack. Wasn't that where Redmawnachu hid . . . in cracks in the earth? Wasn't that how it stole people's souls . . . by sucking them down through cracks? *Wasn't it?*

Billy started to shake. What if the soul stealer was waiting there inches from his toes? What if it was holding its breath, just waiting for him to swing his leg so it could grab hold of him and drink his life?

"Awwwwww," he told himself, "you're acting crazy now. Why would it even bother with me? It's got all the souls in the world to steal."

But, he thought, still . . . it *could* be there.

Kneeling down on the sidewalk, Billy held the history book out in front of him. Slowly, he shoved it forward toward the pebble.

Inch after inch, he moved the book closer to the pebble. Billy was so scared that he could barely breathe. His hands were shaking so badly that he could hardly hold on to the book.

Ever so slowly, the corner of the book drew closer toward the pebble.

Toward the crack.

Four inches away from it.

Three inches away.

Two . . .

And then, suddenly, the air filled with a thick burning smell. Billy screamed. He threw himself

79

backward, falling away from the pebble, from the crack.

The history book dropped out of his hands. It fell forward, right over the crack in the sidewalk.

But it didn't just lie there.

It bounced up into the air and flew down the street. As if it had been knocked away.

Billy leaped to his feet. He jumped up and down, afraid to stand still. Where was the soul stealer?

Where?!

I'm here, Billcarne.

Billy screamed again. He heard it. He *heard* it! Redmawnachu's voice . . . it had been in his head. He had heard it speaking to him. Before he could react, before he could think, it spoke to him again.

I am everywhere, Billcarne.

Billy grabbed the history book. Its paper cover was now torn. Little pieces of dirt and stone were stuck to it. Billy didn't notice.

And I am going to get you, Billcarne.

Billy stood in the center of the block of sidewalk. He was too terrified to scream again. He was too terrified to move. All he could do was hug the history book to him like a shield. And stand in the center of the cement square.

Soon, Billcarne.
And shake.
Very, very hard.
Very soon.

Billy sat in the pew at church the next day alongside his parents. When the moment came for silent prayer, he certainly felt like praying. The problem was, he didn't know what he should pray for.

Which prayer would be the most important? he wondered. Should I pray that everyone stops thinking I'm crazy? Or to get my friends back? Or for everyone to believe me? What?

What?

Billy looked around the church. He wondered if people were still staring at him as they had been yesterday. He stopped looking around when he found that they were.

Maybe I shouldn't even care about anyone else, he thought. Maybe I should just pray that I don't get eaten by that thing when it finally starts killing people again, like it killed all those Indians.

And then a different thought entered Billy's head.

Maybe I should just pray that I really am crazy.

Billy bowed his head and shut his eyes. As he did, he thought, If I did that, I mean, if I *was* crazy, then at least everyone else would be safe.

Billy opened his eyes again. Turning his head just a little, he peeked at his mother and then his father. He felt so confused, so helpless. He had thought that he might find the answers he was looking for in church.

So far nothing had happened to give him any answers.

Even the minister's sermon had been no help. Billy had thought it might at the beginning. When the minister had first started talking, it had seemed that he was talking straight to Billy.

"People ask God for things all the time. Did you know that? All the time. Whenever they're lost, or frightened, or confused—whenever they've got a problem that's too big for them— who do they turn to? Why, God . . . of course."

The opening of his sermon had caught Billy's attention right away. The scared boy listened closely as the minister went on, hoping for an answer to his problem.

"No matter what happens in this life, there's always someone who will look to God for the way out of their problems. God, my baby is sick. God, my car isn't running right. God, I need more money. God, I wish my boyfriend wasn't such a jerk. God, can't you get something good on television? God, don't let it rain today—I want to go on a picnic."

The minister slapped his hand down on his pulpit.

"No, God—don't let it rain today. I want to go on a picnic. Don't feed the Earth. Don't take care of the forests that give us oxygen. Don't water the crops we need to eat. Don't worry about any of that . . . Don't worry about anyone but *me,* Lord. I want to go on a picnic."

The minister threw up his hands. Raising his voice almost to a roar, he told everyone, "If you ever wondered why God doesn't answer your prayers—that might be the reason. Too many people wasting God's precious time with idiotic prayers like that. Me, me, me. Gimme, gimme, gimme."

The minister took a deep breath. Then, in a voice softer than before, he said, "People, if you want

God's help, you have to earn it. Remember the saying, 'God helps those who help themselves.' "

Billy wondered what he was supposed to do with that advice. He wasn't asking for something stupid. He wanted to stop a monster. He was trying to save everyone from whatever horrible thing was crawling around under Darbenburg.

Is that so much to ask?

He waited for a moment after thinking his question. He hoped that, being there in church, maybe he might get some kind of an answer. But he heard nothing.

Face it, he told himself, as far as this thing goes, it looks like you're on your own.

He let that thought roll around in his brain as he got up with his parents. The services had come to an end. It was time to go home. As everyone moved slowly toward the back of the church, Billy watched them leaving through the large, arched doors.

They looked to him as if they were all walking forward into a gigantic mouth. The mouth of the thing under the grass. Then, suddenly, Billy got very angry at himself.

Well, he thought, that's just great. I'm on my own and I can't do anything. Either there's a seven-hundred-year-old monster crawling around under my town, or I'm just plain nuts.

Billy and his parents reached the doorway. Even though he knew it was only a door, Billy had to force himself to step outside. Part of him knew he had scared himself by thinking of the door as a mouth. Part of him knew that once he was outside, the thing under the ground could get him.

If the monster is real, he thought, then it can suck people down into the ground through any kind of crack. It can move through the earth like a fish through water. And, I guess, if those Indians were right, there's nothing in the world that can stop it.

Billy's dad and mom slowed down to talk with the minister. As they did, Billy thought, And if there is no monster, then I'm a nut job. And sooner or later someone's going to have to put me in the crazy house.

Billy watched his dad talking to the minister. He wondered how long they would talk. He wondered when they would leave. And what they would do afterward.

Would they go out for breakfast? Would they go home?

And, he wondered, will it make any difference?

I mean, who cares? I've got to figure out if this monster thing is real, or if I'm crazy.

And then Billy suddenly noticed a man standing on the sidewalk down in front of the church. Billy noticed him for a number of reasons. The man was arguing with another man. He was loud and waving his arms about as he argued. He was also very heavy.

Billy decided the man would've been hard not to notice—big and fat and loud and waving his arms around.

And then Billy noticed something else.

Suddenly, the air was filled with a thick, burning smell. Before anyone could notice it, however, the fat man gave out a scream. As everyone watched, he grabbed his chest. He kept screaming, telling everyone that he was having a heart attack.

Billy didn't watch the man's waving arms or listen to his screams. Billy watched his feet.

The man was standing directly on the crack between two sections of the sidewalk. And as much as he was screaming and waving his arms, his feet never moved from the crack.

Not until the man fell over.

By that time a lot of people had gathered

around him. Some said they should take his tie off and loosen the top button of his shirt.

Some kept shouting for a doctor. Others said everyone should get back and give him some air. The minister ran back inside the church to call for an ambulance. Even Billy's parents ran down the steps to see what they could do.

But not Billy.

He stayed up on top of the thick stone steps of the church. Watching everyone gather around the fat man, he knew what had happened.

Billy knew that no ambulance was going to reach the church in time to help the man on the ground. He also knew two other things.

First, he knew that the fat man on the sidewalk below was dead.

Second, he knew he did not die of a heart attack.

Billy knew that the man had had his soul stolen by a monster, and that now the whole world was in danger.

He wanted to scream to his parents to come back up on the steps, but he didn't dare. He knew if he did that everyone would think he was crazy. And he couldn't let anyone put him away in a hospital.

He was the only person on Earth who knew

that there was a monster crawling around under the ground.

The only person who knew anything about it at all.

The only person who knew how to tell where it was.

The only person who knew how to stop it.

On the ground in front of the church, everyone kept running around in circles. People tried to keep children away from the fat man's body. Everyone was in a panic, shouting and yelling.

But Billy did not look at any of them. His eyes were watching the grass of the church lawn. As he watched, he could see the grass moving the same way water moved on the surface when a fish was swimming by underneath.

There was no wind.

The leaves on the trees were not moving. The branches of the bushes next to the church were not moving.

The petals of the flowers in the front of the church were not moving.

Nothing was moving except the line of grass that marked the path of the monster.

Well, thought Billy, at least I know I'm not crazy.

And then, as all traces of the thing beneath the

grass disappeared from sight, Billy remembered what the minister had said.

"God helps those who help themselves."

And suddenly Billy knew that there was only one person in the world who could stop the monster.

Billy Carne had finally realized that the only person who could save the world . . . was he.

And only he.

12

BBBRRRRRiiinnngggggg!

The last bell of the school day sounded—time to go home. Billy Carne ran for the door as fast as he could. He had never been happier to hear a bell in all his life. It had been a long, long day.

First, none of the guys had met him to walk to school. Not Mike or Jack. Not Malcomb. Not Danny.

Not even Danny.

It had been a long walk to school without any of his friends. But the day that followed had been a thousand times longer.

A million.

One of his friends—Mike or Jack or Malcomb or Danny—had told someone about the history book. And they had told someone else. And they had told someone else.

Before the end of homeroom, Billy knew that everyone—*everyone*—had heard about the thing under the grass—that everyone was laughing at him. He had never had a worse day in his life.

When the bell rang, Billy was the first on his feet. The first out the door. The first in the hall. He ran for the front door of the school as fast as he could. He didn't want to see anyone. All he wanted to do was get away from everyone and just go home.

But before he could make it out the door, Mr. Knisbaum stepped from his room. Seeing Billy, he put up his hand, signaling the boy to stop. As Billy slowed down, the teacher asked him, "So, Carne—tell me. What did you find out about your monster?"

Mr. Knisbaum walked along with Billy down the hall toward the front door. He didn't say anything, but Billy could tell that he was waiting for an answer.

Billy thought for a long moment before saying anything. Sure—he had discovered plenty. First in the library. All that stuff about the Indians in the history book—he had thought he had found everything he needed. Then he had watched the thing kill a man.

That should be enough proof for *anybody*.

But he hadn't told anyone about that.

Why would I? he asked himself. If I couldn't convince Jack or Mike or Malcomb about this thing, if even *Danny* wouldn't believe me about what I found at the library, there's no way they would've believed that I'd seen the thing come back and kill somebody.

Still, he thought, Mr. Knisbaum had taken an interest in his story on Saturday. He hadn't laughed at him. Had even tried to help him.

And then Billy almost went ahead and told Mr. Knisbaum about what he had seen on Sunday. He wanted to. He wanted to tell *somebody,* and Mr. Knisbaum was the only person in the whole town who hadn't made fun of him or looked at him as if he had grown another head.

But then, just as he started to tell Mr. Knisbaum about what had happened on Sunday, he thought, Oh, man . . . no way. Who am I kidding? No teacher is ever going to believe something as crazy as this.

Billy looked up at Mr. Knisbaum. He wished he could dare to tell him what he really thought. He wanted to shout, Yeah! I found out stuff, all right. I found out that my monster is real—that it's hundreds of years old.

I found out how you can tell where it is and how you can tell when it's coming at you.

Yeah—and then I found out how it kills people because I saw it kill a man right outside church.

He wanted to say all of that really bad. But he was too scared. Billy knew that adults talked to each other, that teachers called parents when they thought they should know something about their kids. With the whole school—heck, with the whole *town*—talking about him, did he really dare say anything that would make him sound even crazier to people?

So, as much as Billy wanted to tell Mr. Knisbaum everything, all he could think of was his father the psychiatrist. And what happened to people who said crazy things. So instead of the truth, he simply said, "Oh, nothing—really."

"Nothing?" asked the teacher, sounding a little surprised. Billy could tell Mr. Knisbaum had heard about what he had told his friends on Saturday . . . just like everyone else. Not knowing what else to do, though, he lied, "Nawwww. I think I just got a little carried away with stuff." Backing toward the front door, he added, "I'm sorry I bothered you and all on Saturday. I guess I was just being kind of dorky."

And then, before the teacher could ask him

anything else, Billy shoved the door open and raced outside. He jumped down the front steps three and four at a time. When he got to the bottom, he spotted his mother's car and headed straight for it.

As he got in, his mother said, "Hey, champ. Right on time." As she turned the key to start the car, she added, "I'm surprised you asked me to pick you up today."

"Yeah. Thanks."

"You're welcome," she told him. Mrs. Carne pulled the car away from the school. As she moved it out into the traffic, she said, "I thought you always walked home with Danny and that other bunch of boys?"

"Not today," Billy answered. Pretending to be looking in one of his books, he added, "I didn't feel like it."

"That's fine," said his mom. She waited a minute, then asked, "But what about that construction over on the South Side? I thought you just *had* to see that every day."

"Nah," he lied to his mother. "It's okay. But I'm kind of sick of it."

Mrs. Carne didn't say or ask Billy anything else. Traffic was a little heavy and she was too busy watching the road. Billy was glad. He didn't know what he would say if his mother was to start asking him any more questions.

Billy was sick from worrying.

He was scared that the thing from under the grass was going to come after him.

He was scared that it was going to kill his parents. That it was going to suck him and them and all his friends under the ground.

That it was going to eat their souls and then kill everyone else in the whole world.

But she *was* his mother.

If anyone would understand, Billy thought, if anyone would take his side—no matter what—it would be his mother. He looked over at her, and suddenly he remembered all the times she had stood up for him, no matter what he had done.

She loved him. He knew it. She would always love him. No matter what he said. No matter what he did.

No matter what.

She *had* to. She was his mom, and that's what moms were supposed to do.

Suddenly, Billy felt a great deal better. He knew he could tell his mother what had happened—all of it—and that she would understand. Billy closed the book he had been pretending to study. And then, just before he could start to talk, his mother said, "Billy . . ."

"Yes, Mom?"

"I just wanted to tell you how happy I am that this monster nonsense seems to be over."

Billy's heart sank. He could hardly believe his ears.

"Your father and I were very worried about what we'd been hearing," his mother told him. "About you saying that there was something under the ground that was going to go around and kill everybody."

What could he do? he wondered hopelessly. What could he do now?

"Your father even thought that, well . . . he even thought that maybe you might need some kind of treatments."

I knew it, thought Billy. *I knew it!* Everyone thinks I'm crazy.

"But I told him not to worry . . . that you'd snap out of it. I told him all these stories we've been hearing were just exaggerations."

The light at the corner ahead changed to red. Billy's mother started slowing the car. She turned the wheel to avoid a small pothole. Then, as they drifted toward the car in front of them, she turned and asked Billy, "They were exaggerations, weren't they, dear?"

"Yeah, sure," Billy answered his mother with a tired voice. He felt very lost at that moment. His mother had been his last hope. Not knowing what else to do, Billy turned around in his seat and stared out the back window.

"What was that, Billy?"

"Nothing, Mom."

Mrs. Carne finally stopped the car. She sat waiting patiently for the light to change. Billy waited, too. But unlike his mother, Billy didn't care when the light changed.

His mother had just told him that she and his father thought he might be crazy.

No, Billy didn't care when the light changed. He didn't care what happened at all.

He was too busy trying not to think about the fact that his own parents were ready to have him taken away.

He was too busy trying not to cry.

In fact, he was so wrapped up in his problems that, for a second, he didn't notice the thick, burning smell coming through the car window.

13

Billy looked up.

"Mom," he said, looking around. "Do you smell that?"

Mrs. Carne didn't want to look away from the road. Even though Billy had spoken in a really loud voice, she didn't answer him. Looking at her, he could tell she wasn't paying any attention to him at all.

And then Billy felt the car move. It was only the tiniest tremor, but it scared him.

Then he felt it again.

"What was that?" asked his mother.

"Mom!" Billy screamed. "Go! Go!"

Mrs. Carne turned her head.

"Billy," she asked. "What are you screaming about? It was just a little shaking. Honestly . . ."

"No, Mom—please. You don't understand. You've got to go—you've got to go *now!*"

The burning smell was filling the car. Even Billy's mother finally noticed it. Holding her hand over her nose, she asked, "My goodness—what is that horrible odor?"

Billy was terrified. The burning smell was getting stronger and stronger.

That pothole, he thought. The monster—it travels through cracks in the earth. Isn't that what a pothole is ... just a big crack in the street?

The monster's in that pothole!

Billy had no doubts. Redmawnachu, the soul stealer, was coming for him.

For him *and his mom!*

Suddenly, Billy realized that his mother was not going to do anything. He knew that if he didn't do something, they were both doomed.

Without thinking, he pushed his way across the front seat. Getting up alongside his mother— even though he hadn't taken off his seatbelt— Billy managed to stamp his foot down on top of hers.

On top of the gas pedal.

Instantly, the car's motor roared.

"Billy!" screamed Mrs. Carne. "Stop! What are you doing? Stop it!"

Billy's mom was afraid of running the red light. Afraid of what would happen if their car ran into someone else's car.

She shouldn't have worried. Even though Billy was grinding his foot into hers as hard as he could . . . *the car didn't go anywhere!*

"He's got us!" shouted Billy.

"Who's got us?" screamed Mrs. Carne. As she pushed against Billy, suddenly the red light changed to green. Horns started honking behind her. Giving her son one final shove, Mrs. Carne pushed him back to his own side of the car.

"I don't know what's gotten into you," said Billy's mother as she tried to move the car forward.

"Don't worry about me," pleaded Billy. "Don't think about it. Just get us out of here!"

Mrs. Carne pressed down on the gas pedal. Still the car did not move forward.

"I don't understand this," she said.

Billy's mother looked in her rearview mirror to see if she could find out what was wrong. All she could see was other drivers shaking their fists at her.

Mrs. Carne did not usually do a great deal of driving. She really did not know a lot about cars.

But she did know something about gravity.

"Billy!" she shouted all of a sudden. "We're sinking!"

"I know, Mom," he yelled back to her. "I know! Please—get us out before it's too late!"

The burning smell was gagging. Billy felt as if he was going to throw up if he had to breathe it for another second. His mother started coughing.

The car slipped again. Billy looked out the back window. The car was starting to tilt downward.

"Mom!" Billy screamed. "We're sinking into the street."

People on the sidewalk started pointing. Some were yelling. Some started looking for a policeman. Inside the car, Billy's mom shouted, "Billy—hang on!"

"Go, Mom—go. Go, GO *GO!*"

Mrs. Carne floored the gas pedal. Billy could feel the back tires spinning. The tires made a hideous, squealing noise, but the car didn't move. Seconds later, a thick gray cloud rose up from the back of the car.

Outside, a man ran up as close as he dared to Mrs. Carne's window.

"Get out of there!" he yelled. "You're in a hole! And it's getting bigger!"

"Mom! It's got us! *Mom!*"

"Hang on, Billy," shouted Mrs. Carne. "Just hang on!"

Billy's mother clutched the steering wheel as if it were a life preserver in a stormy ocean. She turned it first one way, then the other. All the time she kept pumping the gas harder and harder.

Inside the car, Billy could no longer tell the burning smell of the monster from the fresh smell of burning rubber coming from the car's tires. Billy's mother couldn't understand it. The car should have just moved forward.

It was just in a pothole. She was giving the car all the gas it could have possibly needed. There shouldn't have been any problem.

The car should have just ... moved ... forward.

"What's wrong with this stupid car?" she screamed.

The whole car rocked back and forth as Mrs. Carne kept trying to get it out of the hole in the street. She couldn't imagine what was holding it back.

But Billy could.

He knew what it was.

It was the monster from beneath the grass. It was Redmawnachu—the soul stealer. That was

103

what was holding them back. That's what was pulling them down into the hole in the street.

The hole that kept growing larger and larger.

And then, suddenly, just as the light ahead changed back to red, the car's tires bit into something solid. It was just for the briefest second, but that was all that was needed. Mrs. Carne screamed as her car surged forward. Billy screamed with her.

The car broke free and shot up and out of the hole with a roar. Its tires screeched as it rocketed up and over the lip of the hole. For just a moment, all four wheels were actually off the ground!

And then the car landed.

Hard!

The first tire to hit was the one in the front on the left-hand side. The right front tire hit a split-second later. The car crashed against the street so hard, Billy's teeth jammed together, biting the inside of his mouth.

Then the still-spinning back tires slammed against the ground. The reason they were still spinning was that Billy's mother was so scared, she never took her foot off the gas.

Instantly, the car roared down the street. Before Mrs. Carne could hit the brakes, the car slammed into another car going through the intersection.

Mrs. Carne's head hit the steering wheel. Billy's hit the dashboard. As their car stopped, buried in the side of the one they had hit, both Billy and his mom started to slip into unconsciousness.

Billy tried to fight it. Looking in the mirror outside his window, he could see the hole in the street.

When his mother had first steered around it, the pothole had been only the size of a loaf of bread.

Now it was the size of a truck.

It was getting bigger.

And it was coming directly for their car.

14

"Where am I?"

"Sssssssssshhhhhhhh." A soft voice Billy didn't recognize spoke to him in a whisper. "Don't move. Don't try to talk. You've got to stay quiet now."

Despite what the voice told him, Billy struggled both to rise up out of his bed and to open his eyes. The pain that followed felt like knives being stuck in his head. It felt like someone was going to tear his head off.

It hurt so much that both his eyes filled with tears. But he didn't scream or make a noise of any kind. Instead, he just fought the pain as he asked again, "Where am I?"

Then he collapsed. He had to shut his eyes. The pain from the lights was simply too much for him. Falling back into his pillows, he pulled in a deep breath and asked, "Where's my mom? What happened?"

"Sssssshhhhhhh," came the soft voice again. "I'll tell you everything that happened, but you've got to stay quiet and get your rest."

Billy made a noise that sounded like "Okay." It was the best he could do. He really *was* tired.

But . . . he had to know what had happened.

He *had* to.

"My name is Mrs. Sipowitz," the voice identified itself. "I'm a nurse here at the hospital. They brought you here a few hours ago. Your mother is here, too."

Billy started to ask another question, but Mrs. Sipowitz put her fingers to his lips.

"Yes, your mother is all right. She hit her head harder than you did, so she'll probably have to stay here a bit longer than you will. But basically the two of you are both okay. You just got banged up a bit."

"That's all?" croaked Billy. His mouth was dry. It felt hot and fuzzy. Somehow knowing how he felt, the nurse put a cup of cold water in Billy's hand and then said softly, "Drink." As he raised the cup to his mouth, she told him, "And, yes— even though your car was pretty well totalled, the two of you came through it without any broken bones or long-lasting damage."

"Can I see her?"

"Not until tomorrow. Your mother is sleeping and shouldn't be disturbed. And you, young man, shouldn't be moving around, either."

The nurse took hold of Billy's wrist. He knew she was taking his pulse. She kept talking as she did so, telling him, "And I mean it. You might feel all right just lying there, but if you try getting out of that bed you'll get the granddaddy of all headaches."

Mrs. Sipowitz went to the door. Her hand on the knob, she turned back and said, "Now. You listen to me, Billy. You're doing fine. You got roughed up. You had a close call. But you and your mom are both okay, and you'll be back home and back to normal in no time. All right?"

"Yeah. Thanks." Then, just as the nurse was ready to leave, Billy asked, "Did you hear anything about what happened? I mean, where the hole came from?"

"No. It was on the news, but no one knows what happened. The street just caved in somehow. But, you know how it is . . . everyone's blaming someone else. The city says that the street was in perfect shape and that it was impossible for it to collapse. But . . ."

"But," said Billy, his throat not hurting so badly after his drink, "there's this big, car-swallowing hole in the middle of Munsen Street that says they're wrong."

"Yes," agreed Mrs. Sipowitz. "Something like that."

"So," Billy asked in a curious voice, "no one saw anything strange, or anything?"

"Not that I heard about," answered the nurse. And then the door closed behind her, and Billy was alone again.

Alone in the darkness.

Billy turned over in bed. It hurt a little to do so, but he didn't want to look at the closed door. It made him feel trapped in the hospital room.

But you are *trapped, Billcarne.*

Billy jumped. That hurt, too, but he didn't even notice the pain. He was too scared.

"What do you want?" he whispered. Billy didn't know how he could hear the monster. He didn't care. Billy figured it was something like on "Star Trek" where some of the aliens could talk to each other just by thinking.

I want your soul, Billcarne.

"Sorry," Billy whispered to the voice that only he could hear. "I'm still using it."

Not for long, Billcarne. Soon it will be mine. Tasty treat to suck on.

"Good luck, ugly."

Billy swallowed. It hurt. His throat had gone dry from fear. He could feel the monster from under the grass in his brain. The thing was laughing at him. Angry, Billy spoke out loud.

"Go ahead. Laugh. You missed me today and you missed me yesterday and you missed me the day before that. And you know what, I bet you'll keep right on missing me, too."

Foolish puppy you are, Billcarne. You were the first being I spied upon my return to the surface world. I have been playing with you. Teasing you.

"Yeah, right," growled Billy. He was afraid that the monster was telling the truth. But whether it was or not, it didn't matter.

Deep inside himself, Billy knew he had to do something. His dad had always told him that a person has to confront his fears. Billy thought to himself, Well, if there was ever anything in this world that I was afraid of, this thing is it.

So, do as your father has instructed, puppy. Confront me, Billcarne.

"I hate you!" Billy shouted.

What does that matter?

Billy put his hands over his ears. He hated the sound of the monster's voice in his head. It felt as if someone had poured cold grease inside his skull.

Hate me. Fear me. In the end, Billcarne, all you will do is feed me.

"Hey, no way José," Billy whispered. "You can't get me. I'm way up here in the hospital. You can only get people on the ground."

You will have to come out sometime, Billcarne. I have great patience. I can wait.

"I don't ever have to come out," Billy lied. "I can stay in here forever."

Then I will steal your mother's soul.

"Ha," Billy laughed. "She's in here, too. You can't get her, either."

Then your father. Your friends. Everyone. Redmawnachu's oily voice chuckled within Billy's head. *I will eat the rest of the souls in the world.*

"No way," Billy whispered.

Yes. I will. You and your mother may stay where you are. I will dine on all the billions of other souls on this Earth of yours. And then I will leave your world and move on to the next. And the next. And the next.

"No."

Yes. It is what I have done since the beginning of time. It is my way. I have stayed on this planet far too long. I have played with you, Billcarne, because it amused me to do so. But now I will strip this world of souls and be on my way.

"You're a chicken."

I am a small bird? Why would you say this to me?

Billy realized that the thing from beneath the grass did not understand him. Part of him felt relief that the monster was saying that it was going away. But a big part of him was more scared than ever.

Redmawnachu said it was going to kill Billy's father. His father and then everyone else in the world. Billy knew he was the only person in the entire world who had a chance to stop the soul stealer.

The creature had said that Billy was the first person he had seen since the Indians. It had told him that it had been teasing him. Like a cat would a mouse.

But now the monster was bored, and was ready to move on. If Billy let him leave, it meant the end of everything.

Everything.

Redmawnachu would steal the souls from

every person he'd ever known. From every person in the entire world. From all the dogs and cows and bears and everything that walked. Maybe even from the trees and grass.

The only chance anyone has, thought Billy, is if I stop it.

Oh, came Redmawnachu's voice in his head again. *And how would you do that?*

"I called you a chicken before," Billy said. He was so afraid. He wasn't sure he could go ahead with what he was thinking. The monster could read his mind, but . . .

It only seems to read the *front* of my mind. The thought gave Billy hope. The stuff I keep in the back of my mind . . . *that it doesn't seem to be able to hear.*

Crossing his fingers for luck, Billy said, "Calling someone chicken means you think they're a coward. And that's what you are. You're a coward."

What makes you think so, Billcarne?

"Because," Billy answered, "you know I could kick your butt if you had the guts to fight me."

The monster's voice did not return to Billy's head. For a moment, Billy wondered what had happened to it. Then, suddenly, the building began to shake.

113

Billy grabbed on to his bed. It bounced around the room as the walls began vibrating.

Plaster broke loose from the ceiling. Cracks formed in the walls and along the ceiling. Dust fell from the cracks, forming a gray cloud.

The lights flickered off and on—both in Billy's room and out in the hallway. Billy could hear people screaming all through the hospital.

Then the vibrations stopped. Billy's bed stopped bouncing up and down. The lights came back on and stayed on. Most of the screaming died down.

And the sound of Redmawnachu's voice filled Billy's head once more.

Only here! Only on this terrible world has anyone dared to call me so! This is my strength, Billcarne. Do you think this the strength of a coward?

"I'm the one you want," Billy whispered. "If you don't have the guts to face me, then go on. Go ahead. Kill everybody else and leave."

Billy crossed his fingers. He was really scared. But he knew from what Redmawnachu had just told him that one of the Taranka Indians must have done the same thing to him that Billy had just done. And they had managed to trap him for hundreds of years.

Pushing his fear to the back of his mind, Billy

114

took a deep breath, and then he said, "But whenever you get to that next planet—you remember that you *ran!* Remember that! Remember that you ran away from Billy Carne!"

The walls shook again—twice as bad as the last time. More dust fell from above. Billy could hear things crashing outside his room. More people screamed. Billy put his hands over his head, afraid the ceiling was going to fall on him.

But then the tremor stopped, and Redmawnachu's voice came once more.

Very well, I will wait for you, Billcarne. I will wait one day. Then, if you have not come to me, it will be you who is the coward.

Billy sat shaking in his bed.

Then I will steal all the souls of your world and leave you behind.

He had just challenged a monster that had lived since the beginning of time to a duel.

One day, Billcarne.

With the lives of everyone in the entire world— six billion souls—as the prize.

Only one day.

Sweat was running down Billy's face. He was so scared he could barely breathe. What could he do? What?

No one believes me. Even if I tell them everything, show them everything that happened . . . they'll all just think I'm a little kid. A *nutty* little kid.

Billy Carne had a big problem. He had to face the greatest, most terrible monster in the entire universe.

By himself.

Tomorrow.

It did not look good.

And then the door to Billy's room opened. He jumped at the sound, thinking for a second that Redmawnachu had come for him. When he turned, however, he saw that it was Mr. Knisbaum. The teacher was covered with dust and plaster. Billy could tell from looking at his clothing that he had fallen down several times coming to his room.

"Mr. Knisbaum," said Billy with surprise in his voice. "What are you doing here?"

"Came to see you," he answered. He looked around the room at all the damage for a moment, then said, "Looks like you sure know how to make some bad enemies."

Billy's eyes popped. Mr. Knisbaum *knew*. He *understood*. He *knew,* and he'd come to help. At least Billy hoped he had. More nervous than ever, the boy asked, "Mr. Knisbaum . . . what do you mean?"

"I mean I've been checking around and . . . unless I miss my guess . . . you've got a monster named Redmawnachu chasing you. Now, what are the two of us going to do about it?"

He *believes* me! thought Billy. He *believes* me!

Suddenly, Billy Carne was no longer afraid. He didn't have time to be afraid.

He had work to do.

15

"I'm still in the hospital, I'm still in the hospital, I'm still in the hospital . . ."

"Just keep saying it over and over, Carne," said Mr. Knisbaum. "Over and over."

The teacher kept driving through the darkness. Billy kept repeating the same sentence again and again.

In the back of his mind, he thought about everything that had happened since that afternoon.

Mr. Knisbaum had told him a lot.

He had heard about the hole that had almost swallowed Billy and his mom. He had gone to see it. When he was there, he had talked to all the officials he could find.

Mr. Knisbaum told Billy that the police and the city workers had all agreed. Billy's mom's car hadn't done anything to the street. No car could have.

They also told him that the street had not collapsed. There were no sewers under that part of the street, no faults or caves or anything. As far as the city was concerned, it should have been impossible for the street to collapse.

After that, Mr. Knisbaum said that he had gone back to the library and asked about the books Billy had taken out. When he found that Billy had taken out only one book, and that he had already returned it, he asked if he could see that book as well.

The history of Darbenburg.

And, after he had read that book, he knew what Billy knew. He also knew he had to get to Billy as quickly as he could and find out what was going on.

Billy was glad he had.

He and Mr. Knisbaum talked for a long time. No one came to chase the teacher away. All the nurses and doctors were too busy trying to calm down all their patients after Redmawnachu shook the whole hospital.

After Mr. Knisbaum told Billy everything he had done, he admitted, "I have to tell you, I didn't really know if I believed in a monster that could run around underneath the ground and suck people's souls out of their bodies ... even after seeing the hole in Munsen Street. But after what just happened here . . . Oh, man, do I believe."

"Yeah," Billy had said. "The problem is going to be getting anyone else to believe us."

"Yes, Carne," agreed Mr. Knisbaum, "that is the problem."

The two talked for a long time then about what they could do to stop Redmawnachu. Mr. Knisbaum told Billy that he had talked to lots of people in the crowd, but no one had seen anything inside the hole in the street.

It seemed strange to both Billy and Mr. Knisbaum. You would think that someone would have seen something. But that wasn't important. Not really.

The only important thing was stopping the soul stealer. Both Billy and Mr. Knisbaum agreed. Even if it meant their lives . . . nothing was more important than stopping Redmawnachu.

The pair had talked about all the things they could try to do. The problem was, though, that almost all their ideas involved getting someone else to believe their story. And they knew that they'd never be able to do that.

Not in less than one day.

Everyone would want to wait. They'd want to

study the problem. They'd want to study Billy and Mr. Knisbaum.

But the thing beneath the grass had said it would wait only one day. And then it would start attacking everyone else in the world.

In the end, Billy and Mr. Knisbaum could think of only one plan that didn't involve anyone else. So, of course, that was the one they used.

First, Mr. Knisbaum went out and took his car around to the back of the hospital. Then he snuck back inside and got Billy. The two of them ran down the back stairs and got outside as fast as they could.

When they piled into the car, Mr. Knisbaum was out of breath. He sat behind the steering wheel, puffing hard. Billy almost laughed. The teacher turned around to him and said, "Go ahead—laugh, Carne. Then you'll have two monsters looking to kill you."

Billy smiled. Mr. Knisbaum pretended to be mad, which made Billy start laughing. He had been sad for so long, he thought he might have forgotten how to laugh. He was glad to see he hadn't.

As Mr. Knisbaum started his car again, he said, "Okay—like we said, start talking about being in the hospital. Don't think about anything else except being in your hospital bed. If that thing is reading your mind, don't think about the plan. We don't want it catching us out in the open."

"I'm still in the hospital," said Billy. Instantly, he said it again. "I'm still in the hospital, I'm still in the hospital, I'm still in . . ."

The sun started to peek out from behind the horizon just as Mr. Knisbaum turned his car onto Morgan Lane. Billy kept chanting his sentence. In just a few more blocks they would be on the South Side of town. More specifically, they would be at the construction site where all the new buildings were going up.

They had chosen that area for a number of reasons.

For one, there wouldn't be anyone else around. The entire area was deserted because everything was being torn down so new things could be put up. And if there was no one around, there was no one else who could get hurt.

Also, Redmawnachu needed souls for energy. If there was no one else around, then there were no other souls around. If the soul stealer came to the South Side of Darbenburg to get Billy, he and Mr. Knisbaum would be the only people the monster could possibly get.

122

If they could just stay out of its way, though . . . if they could just keep it busy. If they could just trick it long enough to tire it out . . .

"Almost there, Billy," said Mr. Knisbaum.

"I'm still at the hospital, I'm still at the hospital . . ."

No, came an oily voice in both their heads, *you're not.*

And then the air was filled with a thick burning smell.

Mr. Knisbaum jerked the wheel to the left. His car spun wildly. As Billy held on to the dashboard, Mr. Knisbaum bounced his car up onto the sidewalk.

BBAAAMMMMM!

The car slammed down on the sidewalk, one side scraping all the buildings, the other getting torn up by the street signs and parking meters and light poles it kept hitting.

Nice trick, the oily voice told them. *Nice try.*

The hole in the center of Morgan Lane split off to the left, toward the sidewalk. It ripped into the concrete slabs and then started speeding after Mr. Knisbaum's car.

"It's chasing us!" screamed Billy.

"Worse than that," said Mr. Knisbaum, watching the approaching crack in his rearview mirror. "It's catching us."

"What'll we do?"

Coming to the end of the block, Mr. Knisbaum drove off the curb and out into the street. Then, just as the hole passed them and broke open ahead of the car, he turned the wheel sharply to the right and went off down the cross street.

Billy shouted in surprise. Behind them, the street began to cave in. Whatever Redmawnachu was, it had the power to pull down the entire intersection. Then a wedge of the crack splintered off and began once more to chase the car.

"What'll we do?"

Mr. Knisbaum pushed his car as hard as he could. He made the next two right turns as fast as possible, trying to put some distance between them and the monster. As he tore down the next street, he told Billy, "That thing seems to like chasing the car. Okay—I'll give him a chase." After making another turn, he told Billy, "Okay, after I make the next turn, we'll be at the construction site. You're getting out there. With luck, that thing will just keep chasing me until it's tired out."

Billy tried to argue, but Mr. Knisbaum wouldn't listen. When he made the next turn, he jammed on the brakes, pushed Billy out of the car, and then tore off down the road. Billy hid behind a large hill of sand next to the cinder blocks the workers had been using the week before.

Sure enough, as he peeked out from his hiding place, he saw the crack round the corner and tear straight down the center of the road. The burning smell filled the air as the road fell apart next to where Billy was hiding. Then the horrible odor faded as the crack smashed its way down the road after Mr. Knisbaum's car.

Standing up, Billy stepped out from behind the sand to get a look at the horror that had been tormenting him for so long. He knew it was crazy—dangerous—but Billy didn't care.

He simply had to see what Redmawnachu looked like.

And so he looked down into the fast-moving, ever-expanding crack. But he didn't see anything.

There was nothing to see.

Billy had imagined a million different shapes and sizes for the terrible thing from beneath the grass. He had seen the monster as having claws, eighty legs, tentacles, armor, spikes, fins—everything and anything. He had thought of it as being every possible color.

But he had not thought of it as having *no* color at all. He hadn't thought of it being invisible.

Foolish puppy, the oily voice slid into Billy's head. *I am not* in *the crack. I* am *the crack.*

And then, just as Mr. Knisbaum's car had almost rounded the next corner, Redmawnachu caught up to it.

Before Billy's eyes, the front end of the car suddenly jerked down below the level of the street. Then the car disappeared entirely. Flames shot up out of the hole, choked by clouds of thick, black smoke.

And now, Billcarne . . . you are mine.

17

Billy turned and ran back to the sand pile. Immediately, the crack doubled back down the road toward him. Terrified, Billy started to climb the hill of sand.

It got Mr. Knisbaum, he thought, terrified. Now it's going to get me!

Redmawnachu arrived at the base of the sand just as Billy reached the top. The monster opened itself wide. Sand began pouring over the lip of the broken street. The burning smell was everywhere. As Billy stared, the thing told him, *Yes, Billcarne. I am not mere meat, as you. I am a creature that flies through space itself. I am not physical as you are, but a being of pure energy.*

Sand began flowing into Redmawnachu faster and faster.

And when I have added your energy to mine, I

shall add that of another and another and on and on until all life on your world is mine.

Billy sat atop the sand pile, shaking with fear. What could he do? The thing from beneath the grass seemed unstoppable. And then Billy asked himself a question.

Why doesn't it just swallow me up and get it over with?

Billy opened his eyes. Suddenly, he had hope again.

Why *doesn't* it just swallow me up?

And then Billy remembered his own plan.

Because . . . it *can't!* We *did* make it tired. It can't go on forever. We were right to bring it down here. With no one else around, it has to get me or it's going to end up hibernating again like when the Taranka chief beat it.

And, once I have all of that, I will have the energy to surge outward to the next world—and that world, too, shall be mine.

Billy stood up and stared down into the crack.

"Yeah, well, I've said it before, and I'll say it again. Good luck, ugly."

Billy stared at the pile of cinder bricks a few feet away from the shrinking sand pile. Then, suddenly—

NO!

Billy jumped. He landed badly on the blocks, tearing his pants and ripping open his knee. But he didn't care. He knew the answer now.

Come back, Billcarne. You cannot escape me.

All he had to do was stay ahead of the monster. Backing away from the edge of the cinder block stack, Billy choked as he saw the first row of bricks topple over. He continued to back away as the second row fell away from sight.

Then the third. And the fourth. And the fifth.

Billy kept backing up, but he started to worry. He was almost out of cinder blocks, but Redmawnachu just kept coming. Desperately, Billy looked around for some other way to escape the thing from beneath the grass.

He didn't see anything that could help him. Most of the buildings that were still standing were too far away. He could never reach any of them in time. What else was in sight—two cement trucks, a few dumpsters, the tower crane, some portable toilets . . .

The crane!

Without thinking, Billy leaped down from the back of the cinder blocks and ran for the crane. It was five stories tall, hundreds of feet wide and long. It weighed tons and tons.

Redmawnachu couldn't possibly swallow that, thought Billy.

Could he?

The ripping crack tore under the remaining cinder blocks. It chased Billy across the open square. Billy ran as hard as he could. His knee hurt very badly, but he didn't care. He just kept running.

Billy didn't bother to waste time looking behind him, either. He knew the monster was coming. He could hear the street caving in behind him— could hear cement and asphalt breaking, flying up into the sky, crashing back down. He could tell the thing from beneath the grass was getting closer.

But the crane was only twenty feet away, so he just kept running.

Just twenty feet! That was all!

But Redmawnachu was right behind him. Maybe only inches from his heels. Billy kept running.

The crane was only twelve feet away.

Billy ran harder. His feet pounded against the pavement.

Eight feet.

Five feet.

Three.

Stop, Billcarne. You are mine!

Billy jumped upward and forward at the same time. The crack split open the street beneath him. Billy sailed through the air for a second, then slammed into the side of the crane's gigantic tread. Quickly, he pulled himself up on top of it. In another second he was up next to the operator's cab.

Now, Billcarne, you have nowhere else to go. Now the chase ends. Now I have you.

Billy held on to the safety clamp next to the cabin door. A moment later, the crane began to shake. Then it began to sway. Looking over the edge, Billy saw that the monster was swallowing the whole crane.

All around the base of the crane, Redmawnachu had begun opening the street to the point where it was going to be able to bring down the entire crane. Slowly, the massive machine began to sink below the level of the street.

Billy looked down. He could see the edges of the street coming closer and closer. The monster was taking no chances, however. Billy could see there was no way he could jump from the crane to the edge of the street.

Which meant the only way he could go was up!

Instantly, Billy clambered up on top of the op-

132

erator's cabin. Redmawnachu read Billy's mind. It knew what he was doing.

It is over, Billcarne. You cannot escape me.

"I can try," Billy whispered.

Without stopping, he moved out from the cab to the tower crane itself. As the base of the machine sank lower and lower, Billy made his way up the five stories of the crane arm. Inch by inch. It was hard going. The entire crane kept bouncing and shaking as the ground continued to evaporate beneath it.

Then, suddenly, Billy almost lost his grip as the crane's heavy hook broke free.

The hook swung out wildly. It whipped back and forth past Billy several times. Each time it came closer to him. Closer and closer. Finally, it grazed his back, tearing his jacket. Billy knew that the next time it returned, it would knock him off the tower.

Then, just before it could come back again, it crashed into the remains of the last building the construction workers had been tearing down. The hook smashed through the building's outer wall, but never came back out. It was stuck inside.

Billy sighed with relief. His leg was still bleeding from when he had landed on the cinder blocks. It hurt a lot, but he didn't care. His back felt wet from where the hook had grazed him. His nose was bleeding, too. He ignored all of it. The only thing that was important was to climb.

And to keep climbing.

Billy turned his head to look below him. The cabin of the crane had started to disappear into the darkness of the gaping crack below him. Billy tried not to think about it and went back to climbing. Hand over hand. Hand over hand.

His fingers ached from his climbing. They were cut in a dozen places. They hurt worse than they ever had before. His head still hurt from the accident. In fact, all of him hurt. Billy had begun to hurt all over.

Stop fighting it, Billcarne. You are mine.

"No way!" Billy screamed. He started climbing again. Higher and higher. Beneath him, the first two stories of the crane had vanished beneath the edge of the street, but Billy kept on climbing.

He made it more than halfway up the crane tower when his sides started to hurt. It was a small pain, but he knew what it meant. He was getting tired. Stopping where he was, he took a deep breath to try to rest.

Instantly, the burning smell of the thing below reached him. Then smoke from Mr. Knisbaum's car went past his head. He coughed from swal-

lowing some of the smoke, then he realized,
Smoke—people will see it! They'll come here.

Billy knew he couldn't rest. He had to keep
moving, had to keep Redmawnachu busy—busy
chasing him.

Billy was almost to the top of the crane tower
when, suddenly, the crane dropped nearly thirty
feet at one time! The crack had burst wide open
in an attempt to swallow the entire crane in
one gulp.

Billy hung on as hard as he could as the giant
machine slammed down. When he opened his
eyes, Billy saw that he was almost below the
level of the street!

He started climbing again—fast. He ignored
his bloody nose. He ignored the pain in his side.
He ignored everything except the fact that the
killer of a million worlds was chasing him.

Then Billy reached the top of the tower. He
shook with fear. What could he do? The crane was
still sinking into the ground, Redmawnachu had
swallowed almost the entire five stories of it . . .
and *still* it was sinking.

*A few more feet, Billcarne. A few more seconds,
and it is all over.*

Billy looked at the heavy cable stretching away
from the top of the tower. When the crane's hook

135

had broken away from the tower before, it had wedged itself inside one of the old South Side buildings that hadn't been torn down yet.

If he could climb it . . . he might still have a chance.

Might.

Rubbing his aching hands together, Billy whispered, "Well, Danny, you were wondering why a guy would ever need to know how to climb a rope . . ." Billy grabbed the thick cable and started to pull himself upward. "Here's one good reason."

Billy locked his legs around the cable and started pulling himself upward. True, he had climbed the rope at school with ease. But it had been made for climbing. The crane cable hadn't. Worse yet, at school he had been rested, ready for the climb.

Now he was tired. Bleeding. He had been in a car wreck and in the hospital until just a few hours ago. His arms felt like lead.

You cannot do this, Billcarne.

And then the crack began to close!

Billy started dragging himself upward as fast as he could. The cable was greasy in spots. He could barely hold on to parts of it. But he kept climbing.

Beneath him, however, the crack kept closing.

When Billy dared to turn and look, he saw that the edges of it were only ten feet apart. He could no longer see the crane. Not even the tower. All he could see was the cable he was climbing, snaking up out of the black hole in the street.

And then the crack closed.

The tower cable was cut in two like spaghetti.

Without the sinking crane to anchor it, the cable went flopping toward the building its hook was stuck in—dragging Billy with it.

BBBAAAAAMMMMMMM!

Billy hit the side of the old building. He hit so hard, he screamed. He hit so hard, tears popped out of his eyes.

Will get . . . you . . . Billcarne.

Billy couldn't believe it. *How* could the monster still be coming for him? *How* could it still have any energy left? After everything it had done— hadn't he tricked it into using itself up? *Hadn't he?!*

Not . . . yet . . . Billcarne.

At the spot where the crack had cut the crane cable in two, a break formed in the street. A break that started moving toward the building from which Billy was hanging. Yard by yard, foot by foot, the horror from beneath the grass was coming for him—*again!*

Billy tried to climb, but he couldn't. His arms hurt too badly. He was too tired. Too scared. What was the point? Nothing could stop the crack. Nothing.

And then Billy remembered Mr. Worster talking to him from the floor as he had made his way to the gymnasium ceiling.

"That's it, Mr. Carne," he had said. "You can do this. Just one hand after another. Breathe and climb."

Breathe and climb.

Billy sucked down a deep breath and then, ignoring his pain, he started climbing again. One hand after another. One hand after another.

Then, as Billy began moving once more, he wondered why the crack had not caught up to him while he had simply been hanging. Looking down, he noticed that the crack was not traveling with the car-chasing speed it had been moving with earlier.

It's going slower! thought Billy. It's slowing down!

Billy kept climbing. Suddenly, he had hope again. Redmawnachu had pushed its game too far. It had been too proud—had insisted on making a prize out of Billy's soul. Now it was running out of power.

But it had not run out yet.

As Billy kept climbing, he could hear the crack getting closer to the building. And then, as Billy looked down again, he saw the split break the curb, shatter the sidewalk, and start grinding its way up the side of the building!

The tip of the crack reached the second floor just as Billy reached the top of the cable. With all his remaining strength, he pulled himself inside the old building.

The crack continued shattering its way upward. Even though it was losing power, it broke through the third floor and kept on moving up.

Billy was gasping. He could barely breathe. He had no strength left. Struggling just to turn himself around, he managed to stick his head out of the hole he had just climbed in through. Staring down the outside wall, he could see the crack . . . three stories away . . .

Coming for him.

Billy backed away from the hole. He was shoving himself across the floor with his feet and elbows. Dragging himself. He didn't have the strength left to run. He could not even stand . . . but he had to get away.

He had to try.

The whole world was depending on him!

He could hear the bricks of the outer wall shattering, exploding outward as Redmawnachu came for him.

Closer and closer came the exploding sounds. Billy kept dragging himself across the floor, trying to escape.

And then the hole he had crawled through split open! Redmawnachu was in the same room as he was!

Billy hurt so bad. But he kept crawling. He had to.

He *had* to!

You ... are ... mine ... Billcarne.

Billy ran up against a wall. He had nowhere else to go! The crack kept moving toward him.

Slower and slower.

But closer and closer.

Billy shut his eyes.

Mine ... mine ... mine ...

The crack was only inches away ... Billy screamed. He couldn't move. And then Redmawnachu made its last lunge.

The boards of the floor shattered, their edges turning to powder. The air crackled with the burning smell ...

And then . . . nothing.

Billy opened his eyes. One inch from his face . . . the crack had stopped.

For good.

EPILOGUE

That night, Billy left his room at the hospital to go see Mr. Knisbaum in his room. He had thought the teacher had died when his car had disappeared, and that Redmawnachu had stolen his soul before coming after Billy.

But it hadn't. It had left Mr. Knisbaum trapped in his car. It thought it would come back and get him later.

It had been wrong.

The two of them talked about a lot of things. Mr. Knisbaum told Billy how the firefighters had gotten him out of his car just in time and brought him to the hospital.

Billy let Mr. Knisbaum know that he hadn't gotten into any trouble. There had been so much confusion in town that no one had noticed Billy had been gone. It had been easy for him to get back into his room without anyone seeing him. Then he blamed his fresh bruises and scrapes and cuts on the earthquake Redmawnachu had caused at the hospital the night before.

"It's true, Mr. K.," said Billy. "There was so much confusion here, no one even missed me."

"So, Carne," asked Mr. Knisbaum, "no one knows about what we did, and no one knows why half the South Side looks like a disaster area?"

"Nope," answered Billy. "The news is talking about the way the street broke under my mom's car, and then the stuff here at the hospital last night, and everything this morning like it was all one big natural string of things."

The two looked at each other for a long moment. Finally, Mr. Knisbaum asked, "So, are you going to tell anyone what happened?"

"I don't know." Billy thought for a moment, then asked, "Are you?"

"Hey . . . what'd I do? I went for a drive. You're the big monster hunter."

Billy smiled. It was true. Even though he hadn't wanted to take on the greatest killer in the galaxy . . . he had.

And he had won.

It made him feel good. He understood how his parents and friends and everyone had felt. They hadn't seen what he had seen, felt what he had felt. The thing from beneath the grass hadn't talked to them. Only to him.

It had challenged only him.

And he had beaten it.

Billy Carne was feeling pretty sure of himself.

In fact, he was thinking that he might even ask Sheila Knisbaum out to the movies after all.

Sure, her dad might be the toughest teacher in the school . . . but he'd seen scarier.

A lot scarier.

Below the hospital . . . deep below all of Darbenburg . . . a presence stirred. It was tired, too tired to do anything today, or even tomorrow.

But someday, it thought, it would move again. In ten years, or a hundred, or a thousand . . . someday it would reach upward once more. Someday it would be free again. Free to stalk the Earth.

And that time, it would make no mistakes.

Until then, however . . . it would be waiting . . . patiently resting. Someday, it told itself, it would be free again.

But for now, it was so tired.

So very tired.

Now it would sleep. In all its billion years, it had

144

never used its energy as it had chasing the Bill-carne. It had never felt the pain it felt now.

Not even after it had been tricked by the chief of the Tarankan tribe. At least that day, it had fed.

But now . . . it had nothing left.

Nothing.

Deep beneath Darbenburg, the thing from under the grass suddenly realized the truth. It was lying if it thought it would ever see the surface again. It would *not* return to the surface. It would not hunt once more.

It was not about to sleep. It was dying.

And knew it.

Struggling within itself to find one last bit of power, the killer of worlds reached upward to the surface, sending its last thought . . .

You . . . win, Billcarne.

Its power fading, the most terrible monster in all the universe felt itself slipping away. It blinked out for a moment, and then came back for one last second.

You . . . win.

And then it disappeared.

Forever.

```
┌───────────────────────────────────┐
│                                   │
│   DARE TO BE SCARED ...           │
│   If *Step On a Crack* made you shiver │
│       from the top of your head   │
│    to the tips of your toes, take a look │
│   at the following nail-biting preview of │
│        *The Dead Kid Did It,*     │
│    the new Avon Camelot Spinetingler │
│        coming in June 1996.       │
│                                   │
└───────────────────────────────────┘
```

I burst into the classroom and screamed, "I just opened my locker, and this dead kid tried to pull me inside!"

For a few seconds everyone looked stunned; then the kids started to laugh. But our teacher, Ms. Kienzle, said, "Dunning Healy, take your seat, and if you ever try that again, you'll be sent to the principal's office. We don't play practical jokes here at Wilson Elementary School."

I started to protest, because it wasn't a joke, but the look on Ms. Kienzle's face told me that you didn't talk back to teachers here, either.

In the two days that I had been at Wilson Elementary, I had already found out that a lot of things were different from my last school. There, we only had one sixth grade teacher. At Wilson we had two, Ms. Kienzle and Mr. Jones, and we alternated between their classes, because the principal, Mr. Crabtree, was trying to get us ready for junior high school.

That was the reason we had lockers, too, just like we would next year, except that for some reason mine had a dead kid in it.

But who was going to believe me now? I wondered. I doubted if anyone in this room would.

When I enrolled I was assigned the only remaining seats, right in the middle of the room, in both Ms. Kienzle's and Mr. Jones's classes. Now I was completely surrounded by fifty eyes staring at me wondering, I was sure, what kind of weirdo I was.

I knew what had happened to me, though. I wasn't making this up.

It all started because I had forgotten to bring my free-reading book to class. When I told Ms. Kienzle about it, she said, "Well, you're new and you're not used to our routine, so yes, you may go out to your locker and get it. But from now on, Dunning, remember that we have free reading on Thursday mornings."

I assured her that I wouldn't forget again.

I left the classroom, rounded the corner, found my locker in the middle of the section, turned the combination lock, and opened the door. I thought I had put by free-reading book on top of my other books, but I didn't see it anywhere.

So I took out all of my schoolbooks and set them on the floor. My free-reading book had fallen to the back of my locker. I reached in to get it, and that's when it happened.

This dead kid grabbed me and tried to pull me inside!

I knew he was dead, because he looked just like all those dead people I'd seen in horror movies. I know what I'm talking about, too, since those are the only kind I rent.

I struggled hard to get out of the kid's grasp— he was really strong—and it took me a couple of minutes, but I finally pulled loose and slammed the locker door. Then I ran as fast as I could back to my classroom to tell Ms. Kienzle. I mean, after all, when you go to school, you don't expect to be

149

pulled into your locker by a dead kid. I just knew she'd do something about it.

Bad idea.

Now all I wanted to do was disappear.

It seemed to take Ms. Kienzle forever to start talking again so that all those eyes wouldn't be staring at me, but she finally did. "Class, I'll give you twenty minutes to go over free-reading books, then we'll have a short period of time when you may each summarize what you read."

I swallowed hard. Oh, no! I couldn't believe it. When was this nightmare going to end? I had brought one of my favorite books from home, *The Cemetery Under the School,* but I didn't want to talk about it in class. I just thought *we* were going to read them. Now, I'd have to tell everyone that I was reading a book about a school that had been built on top of a cemetery and how all kinds of weird things were happening because of it. I'd never live it down. Everyone would believe that all I ever did was think about dead people.

I had already seen some of the books the other kids were reading: *Little Women, The Red Badge of Courage,* and *Light in the Forest.* Oh, well, I thought, at least I was reading what I liked. Those kids were probably reading their books to try and impress Ms. Kienzle.

I opened the book to the first page. I'd read it so many times I could probably quote it word for word, but I never got tired of it.

I had just finished the first paragraph when I felt someone poke me in the back.

Oh, oh, I thought. It's started. I just knew someone was going to make some smart remark about what I had done, so I ignored it.

But the poking continued.

I took a deep breath and slowly turned around, ready to confront whoever it was.

It was a girl. She gave me a quick smile, handed me a note, then looked down at her book.

I turned around quickly and checked to see if Ms. Kienzle had seen what had happened. She hadn't, so I unfolded the note and read:

I believe you. I used to have your locker. The same thing happened to me, too. Let's talk after school.

Kim Barstow

I gulped. I knew I hadn't been making it up, but until this moment I was sure that everyone else in the class had thought I was.

I wrote OKAY at the bottom of the note, then, without looking around, put my hand in the aisle and handed it back to her. She took the note. I heard her opening it.

Well, maybe things were going to work out all right after all, I thought. I could hardly wait to talk to Kim Barstow after school.

IF YOU DARE TO BE SCARED... READ SPINETINGLERS!

by M.T. COFFIN

(#1) THE SUBSTITUTE CREATURE
77829-7/$3.50 US/$4.50 Can

(#2) BILLY BAKER'S DOG WON'T STAY BURIED
77742-8/$3.50 US/$4.50 Can

(#3) MY TEACHER'S A BUG
77785-1/$3.50 US/$4.50 Can

(#4) WHERE HAVE ALL THE PARENTS GONE?
78117-4/$3.50 US/$4.50 Can

(#5) CHECK IT OUT—AND DIE!
78116-6/$3.50 US/$4.50 Can

(#6) SIMON SAYS, "CROAK!"
78232-4/$3.50 US/$4.50 Can

(#7) SNOW DAY
78157-3/$3.50 US/$4.50 Can

(#8) DON'T GO TO THE PRINCIPAL'S OFFICE
78313-4/$3.50 US/$4.99 Can

(#9) STEP ON A CRACK
78432-7/$3.50 US/$4.99 Can

JOIN IN THE ADVENTURES WITH BUNNICULA AND HIS PALS
by James Howe

BUNNICULA   51094-4/ $3.99 US/ $4.99 Can
by James and Deborah Howe

HOWLIDAY INN   69294-5/ $3.99 US/ $5.50 Can

THE CELERY STALKS   69054-3/ $4.50 US/ $6.50 Can
AT MIDNIGHT

NIGHTY-NIGHTMARE   70490-0/ $3.99 US/ $4.99 Can

RETURN TO HOWLIDAY INN
                                       71972-X/ $4.50 US/ $6.50 Can

CREEPY-CRAWLY BIRTHDAY
                                       75984-5/ $5.99 US/ $6.99 Can

THE FRIGHT BEFORE CHRISTMAS
                                       70445-5/ $5.95 US/ $7.50 Can

HOT FUDGE   70610-5/ $5.99 US/ $6.99 Can

SCARED SILLY   70446-3/ $5.99 US/ $6.99 Can

From out of the Shadows...
Stories Filled with Mystery and Suspense by
MARY DOWNING HAHN

TIME FOR ANDREW
72469-3/$4.50 US/$6.50 Can

DAPHNE'S BOOK
72355-7/$4.50 US/$6.50 Can

THE TIME OF THE WITCH
71116-8/ $3.99 US/ $4.99 Can

STEPPING ON THE CRACKS
71900-2/ $3.99 US/ $4.99 Can

THE DEAD MAN IN INDIAN CREEK
71362-4/ $3.99 US/ $4.99 Can

THE DOLL IN THE GARDEN
70865-5/ $4.50 US/ $6.50 Can

FOLLOWING THE MYSTERY MAN
70677-6/ $3.99 US/ $4.99 Can

TALLAHASSEE HIGGINS
70500-1/ $3.99 US/ $4.99 Can

WAIT TILL HELEN COMES
70442-0/ $3.99 US/ $5.50 Can

THE SPANISH KIDNAPPING DISASTER
71712-3/ $3.99 US/ $4.99 Can

THE JELLYFISH SEASON
71635-6/ $3.99 US/ $5.50 Can

THE SARA SUMMER
72354-9/ $3.99 US/ $4.99 Can